One Night in Emerald Creek

A Small Town Romance Novella

Bella Rivers

Copyright © 2023 by Bella Rivers

All rights reserved.

This book is a work of fiction. Names, characters, places and events are the product of the author's imagination. Any resemblance to actual persons, living or dead, events, or places, is purely coincidental.

No portion of this book may be reproduced in any form without written permission from the publisher or author, except as permitted by U.S. copyright law.

ISBN: 978-1-962627-09-2

Developmental editing: Angela James

Copyediting/Proofreading: Grace Wynter, The Writer's Station

Cover design: Echo Grayce, Wildheart Graphics

Contents

1. Thalia — 1
2. Lucas — 13
3. Thalia — 19
4. Lucas — 27
5. Thalia — 31
6. Thalia — 43
7. Thalia — 59
8. Thalia — 69
9. Thalia — 83
10. Lucas — 93
11. Thalia — 103

12.	Thalia	117
13.	Thalia	129
14.	Lucas	141

And so it begins...   151
Alexandra

Afterword   157

About the author   159

Chapter One

Thalia

I lock my front door and step down the frozen steps, my gloved hand holding onto the railing for dear life. Today might decide my career, at least for the next few years. I can't afford to sprain an ankle, or worse.

I'm Hunt Enterprises's youngest architect, yet I've been asked to be the one defending our proposal for a resort renovation out of state. I can't mess this up.

Especially given that I've applied for a promotion, and the water cooler rumor is that I'm shooting out of my range.

So when I received the email last night that the boss's nephew was going to drive me up to Emerald Creek in a company car, I had a moment of panic.

The boss is assigning me a babysitter. Someone to report to him how I'm doing. Tell him if I can handle pressure. How I am with clients. If I'm a good salesperson, not just a creative architect. This is all fair. Nothing to freak out about.

Who are you kidding, Thalia? That's not why you're freaked out.

Yeah, the boss didn't assign me just anyone. He assigned me *Lucas Hunt*.

Hot and cocky Lucas Hunt.

Built like a linebacker, messy blond hair, sparkling green eyes, and a smile that melts all the panties in the office.

Except mine.

I'm not his type, so his smiles are never for me, and besides, he is so out of my league, it's not even funny. So I don't even look his way.

I'm fifteen minutes early, but I'll take standing in the cold against making Lucas Hunt wait for me. Who knows what he might say to me if he has to wait? Once when I was running late to a company-wide meeting, he slowed his steps in the hallway, gestured for me to pass him, and as I was entering the room, leaned in and said, "Wouldn't want you to be the last one in."

I nearly died.

Half the female staff population hated me from then on. The other half gave me sympathetic looks.

My insides still remember the parts of me his gravelly voice brought to life.

But nerds like me, we learn early on what we can crush and where we get crushed. And crushing on the likes of Lucas Hunt? Bad idea. Waste of time.

That's why I stay away.

Until now. And now it's not by choice.

There's a car with the engine running at the curb. Another early riser. I hold back so they don't see me. Who knows who it may be? It's not yet four in the morning. It could be late night for them. They could be drunk. They might be looking for trouble.

The driver's door opens and a silhouette folds out of the car. "Thalia?"

My knees buckle. It's Lucas Hunt. *Or for Chrissakes, Thalia, get a grip. He's hot—get over it.* I throw my shoulders back. "That's me!" I say a little too loud in the deserted street.

I scamper to him, my butt cheeks clamping so I don't slip. It's a trick that actually works. I know I look ridiculous, but who cares? It's not like Lucas is going to notice.

"You okay?" he asks, eyebrows furrowed, one hand extended to guide me to the car.

I have to tilt my head back to look at him. *I'm very much okay. Why?* I open my mouth to answer, but no sound comes out.

His mouth twitches like he's trying not to smile as he guides me to the passenger side. He opens the door for me and swiftly slides the leather backpack I use to carry my files and laptop off my back. *How did he do that?* I normally have to contort myself to get that thing off. The only reason I keep using it is that it was a present from my parents, and also it keeps my hands free. Handrails and all that. "Okay to put this in the back?" he asks, *as he smoothly takes my coat off.*

Again, I open my mouth. "Um...Sure." A sound! At last!

He growls and reaches down, and before I know it, I'm reclined almost horizontally with Lucas Hunt very, very close to me. "You get some sleep now," he says and softly clicks my door closed.

I shut my eyes. This is a nightmare. He slides in the driver's seat and *yup.* Nightmare. His subtle scent of shower gel and clean laundry is impossible to ignore. My eyes flutter open to his muscular forearms flexing inches from my thighs. I shut my eyes tight and roll my head away from him.

Crushing on Lucas might be out of the question, but I'm not dead.

Very much not dead.

Sleep doesn't come, but I still jump out of my bones when a phone rings an hour later through the car's speaker system. *"Carla Highgate calling,"* the robotic voice announces. I straighten my seat as Lucas glances at me. "You okay to take this?" he asks softly.

God, why is he so nice? He's not making things easy for me. I have to keep a level head on this trip. I can't be distracted by Lucas Hunt's scent, his husky voice saying nice things to me, his attentiveness.

Right now, my heartbeat is picking up because of his words, when it should be because of who's calling. My direct boss.

This isn't me.

Women like me, we know to focus on work and only work. Women like my mom and my sister? Different story. They're happy being married to men who make the important decisions for them. At least happy enough to want the same for me.

No thank you.

Plus, it's not like Lucas would want anything to do with me. I just need to scold my body's response to him and refocus on work. This isn't new to me.

There are a lot of hot guys, a lot of hot girls, a lot of hot, happy couples and some maybe less hot but still happy. It just isn't for me. It doesn't mean that in a fantasy world, I wouldn't want this.

But this is the real world.

And in the real world, I've learned to shield myself from the what-ifs. There are certain situations I avoid. Like being in close proximity to the likes of Lucas Hunt. Today isn't one of those days. I'm going to have to deal with that the best I can.

"Sure," I answer him, sounding way more assured than I feel. Or so I hope.

Lucas hits the phone symbol on the screen, and Carla starts talking me through the meeting strategy.

A strategy I put together.

I ahem and uh-huh through our conversation—because what else am I going to do? I'm vying for a promotion to another department, and I'll need her recommendation. I just need to put up with her for another month or two. There's no point in upsetting her now.

I can't help but roll my eyes, though.

And Lucas growls, not even trying to hide his own aggravation.

"What's wrong?" Carla says.

Oh no. "Lucas. That was Lucas. He's um…driving me to Emerald Creek."

"Oh hey, Lucas!" she singsongs, like she's really happy to talk to him. Like he didn't just growl at something she said, something even she has to know was overkill micromanagement. "Be nice to Thalia, okay?"

"I'm always nice," Lucas answers gruffly.

"No bad boy pranks or whatever it is you do all day," she continues in a flirty voice. Carla and I work in design,

Lucas is in construction. And he and his team are one of the best we have, so I'm not sure what she's talking about.

Lucas extends his hand to the console, his scent sending a woosh to my belly. "Bye, Carly."

"You just hung up on her!"

"I'm supposed to be looking out for you. She was pissing you off."

He noticed? But also, *what?* "Says who?"

"Says who what?"

"Who says you're supposed to be looking out for me?" When Mr. Hunt, his uncle, emailed me last night, he said Lucas would join me to *"learn the ropes."* Now, I'm not naïve. There's no way that's the case. But there's even more definitely no way Lucas was sent to look out for me.

"She was pissing you off, right?" Lucas asks in a lazy voice. I glance at him and catch his gaze turned to me, eyes off the road for a beat to read my answer.

Well, yes she was. But I'm not sure how I feel about him stepping in. It's against everything I believe in. And yet, there's a warmth that spreads through my core that says a part of me is very much on board.

I choose not to answer his loaded question.

"My uncle thinks I should learn the ropes of the business with you. Seems to me I could teach you a couple of things too," he adds.

For the next hour or two, I try, and fail, to steer my mind away from the *"couple of things"* Lucas could teach me, none of them having anything to do with Carla.

The GPS indicates we're forty-five minutes away from our destination when Lucas pulls over to a rest stop. "Stay inside while I fill her up. You have the card?"

Our fingers touch briefly when I hand him the expense card, and my mind focuses way too much on that. His hands are strong, calloused from work, warm. Yet his touch sends shivers down my spine.

I need to return my focus to the meeting, and to do that, I slip out of the car to stretch and use the restroom. The cold Vermont air seizes me in a fist of ice. Shivering, I hurry inside.

When I come out of the restroom, Lucas is at the register, my coat on his arm, blocking my exit. "Coffee?" he asks, his eyes doing a body scan.

I'm jittery enough. "No thanks."

He wraps my coat on my shoulders, pulls the lapels close, then seems to decide I need to get my arms in the sleeves. He helps me do just that, but he does it all *facing me.*

I might as well be in his arms, and I nearly die of embarrassment as his warmth and scent shoot straight to my core, electrifying my lady parts in a *very* unprofessional way. *What is wrong with me?*

"Tea? Juice? Water?" he asks as if nothing. As if my body wasn't currently flush against his. I get it, this *is* nothing to him. Girls literally throw themselves at him *all the time*, so having a female against him is just another day at the office for him.

But not for me. Certainly not at the office. Not outside the office either. Not ever.

And why does he have to be so nice and casual about it? Does he not know what he's doing? I look outside to the car, so I don't get lost in his gaze. It's important he doesn't know the effect he has on me. "I'm good, thanks," I clip, trying to sound cool and detached and not at all confused by my reaction to him.

He doesn't move, and I get pushed snug against his warm body by someone squeezing by.

"Granola bar? Muffin?"

My head tilts up, against my better judgment.

"You want that contract, right?" he growls. "You gotta get something in your stomach before the meeting."

"Nope." My stomach is in knots and not just about the meeting. Lucas's babysitting skills aren't helping with the stomach situation. It's been years since someone worried about me being cold or hungry. And it's been...never since I've had my body against a guy like Lucas and wished I could just melt right there.

I really need to get a grip.

Chapter Two

Lucas

There are worse things than being the gofer for the beautiful Thalia Williams.

And if I wasn't so worried about Madison, my younger sister, I'd truthfully enjoy this impromptu getaway with Hunt Enterprises's promising new architect.

Sitting in Emerald Lake Resort's musty conference room, watching her go through the slides of her vision for the renovation of the space, it's hard not to be under her spell.

The fact that she's so clueless about her sexiness is...well, the number one factor in her sexiness.

I couldn't tell you the number of girls at my uncle's firm who do the flipping of the hair, the cute laughs, and whatever else girls do to make guys notice them.

Not Thalia.

If I didn't know better, I'd think I did something for her to dislike me.

But I didn't. So I don't let her dismissive ways get to me. She must be going through some shit. We all are.

I should know.

After my parents died in a car crash that left Madison hospitalized for six months, my life took a one-eighty turn

I was twenty-one, living the happy-go-lucky life of a traveling journeyman, working on various construction sites, here one day, gone the next, a literal jack-of-all-trades.

Mads was sixteen, doing what sixteen-year-old girls do.

Then Mom and Dad were gone, Madison was in the hospital, and I was left alone to take care of her. I was appointed as her guardian.

There was barely any time to mourn our parents. Madison went through multiple surgeries, and then rehab. There was a modest life insurance that helped for a while, but reality caught up fast.

My uncle came through for us, and although I was never his greatest fan, he was supportive. He gave me a job with health benefits for me and mostly Madison, and it's understood that if she's going through shit, I'm missing work to be by her side.

Family always comes first.

Speaking of which, I check my phone again discreetly. No messages from Madison.

Good.

We'll have a late lunch in Emerald Creek, but not at the resort—Thalia said she wanted to get a feel for the town. Something about giving the resort a more local vibe. We'll head home after lunch and should be back in Boston for dinner.

I pocket my phone and relax, letting my eyes wander down Thalia's body while her back is turned to the room and she comments on the slide show.

She really has a perfect body. She's tense right now, as she's been since this morning, her jaw clenching and her knuckles whitening in her lap.

There's a lot at stake for her. A promotion she's hoping to get, into another department, or so I've heard at the office. It would get her out of Carla's grip. I'd like that for her.

But back to her body. She has a petite, curvy frame. A nice round ass, generous tits she insists on hiding under buttoned-up blouses. She always ties her hair up. Most of the time, ponytail. Today, it's rolled up on her nape like a ballet dancer.

Her eyes are a deep, soft brown. Even when she squints at something or someone, there's no meanness, no sarcasm. There might be a question. A confusion she's trying to clear up.

That's how you can tell she's a genuinely good person. She has the kind of eyes that let you right into her soul. It's a tortured, sometimes sad, always rich soul.

One I want to explore, more than her body.

Although her body...

After this meeting, her tension will lower, and hopefully I can get her to loosen up a little. Let me get to know her.

Get her to know me.

I had to beg my uncle for the opportunity, bullshit my way to being with her today. Lie through my teeth over my reasons.

I also had to fight my own guilt at leaving Mads hours away from me. She's had panic attacks in the past, though not in a long time, and it's fucking scary. She needs someone who gets what she's going through and can be there for her.

But she hasn't had one in a while, and Mads is getting annoyed at my hovering over her. When she recently snapped at me to get a life instead of getting into an argument with her, I thought of Thalia.

The truth is, Thalia's been under my skin for months now, and I want an opening. I want her to see me. Notice me.

After I spend a day with her, she won't be able to pretend she doesn't know who I am when I run into her at my uncle's firm.

Look, I know I'm not good enough for her.

She's an architect, and I'm a carpenter. I work with my hands. She has brains.

But a guy can dream, right?

CHAPTER THREE

Thalia

The presentation ends later than planned, but I think it went well. The upper management of the resort was receptive to my vision and asked good questions. I felt a good connection. I don't want to sound overoptimistic, but it seems to me we have the contract.

Too bad Lucas left before the end. Where did he go, anyway? He'd been looking at his phone a lot. *Probably texting a girl*. I wouldn't mind him reporting to his uncle how the GM congratulated me. Now all he's going to see is that my nerves are shot and I'm exhausted. My heart stutters when he exists the building, shaking hands with a man. As he breaks into a jog in the parking lot, I turn around and compose my face in the reflection of the car window.

"What do you think?" I ask as he pulls out of the resort's parking lot.

"You did great."

That's not what I want to know. "D'you think they liked the vision?" *Will they sign with us?* "How did you read their reactions?"

He shoots me a side glance, a slow smirk spreading across his face. "I didn't really look at them."

Great. He was on his phone the whole time? I guess when you're the boss's nephew, you can get away with pretty much anything. I turn my face away from him to hide my disappointment. What was I thinking? He doesn't care about little old Thalia.

Looking out my window, I focus my attention on Emerald Creek. The small town lies on the other side of the lake, nestled in between soft hills, its houses and small buildings hugged tight against one another, a fresh coat of snow glistening on their roofs.

As we approach the covered bridge marking the entrance of Emerald Creek, a black shadow materializes in front of us.

Lucas hits the breaks. The car starts skidding sideways.

I grab the dashboard and look toward the shadow.

It's a cow, jumping across the road, continuing into a field between two houses.

The car keeps sliding toward the bridge.

"Shit," Lucas mutters.

The car stops abruptly and bounces back a foot. My head hits the headrest, and Lucas's arm shoots out across my body, as if to protect me. "Are you alright?" he asks just as water gushes violently ten feet in the air.

"I'm okay. Wh—what was that?"

"Fucking cow came out of nowhere. We hit a fire hydrant." He puts the car in reverse. It makes a screeching noise, jumps back another foot, and stalls in a gruesome ruckus. "Fuck me!"

Water is pooling around us. "Stay in here for now. It's going to freeze real fast," Lucas says as he opens his door.

Fire engine sirens are already sounding in the distance.

I rub my hands together, trying to warm up and comfort myself. We're at a table at The Lazy Salamander, aka Lazy's, the town pub that sits on the town square—The Green, as they call it here. The place is packed. All the tables were taken when we walked in.

But the owner, Justin, seemed to know who we were, and after he shooed his huge, affectionate dog off to sit at the door, a small table materialized out of nowhere, was set for two in record time, and placed strategically right in front of the fireplace, which is presently roaring with an actual fire, the kind that warms your bones and your soul.

Justin himself brings us two heaping plates of beef brisket, today's special. We both needed comfort food after the scare we had. I have to admit, I was glad Lucas was there to handle everything, because I was freaking out.

Granted, he was the one who was driving, but who's to say how I would have reacted if a cow had jumped right in front of us while I was at the wheel?

The bottom line is, Lucas dealt with the mechanic who towed the car to his shop, called the insurance company, carried me out of the car so I wouldn't slip in the freezing puddle, and made sure we have a warm lunch.

Justin sets the plates in front of us. "Sorry to hear what happened to your car. You're in good hands with our mechanic, Colton. He won't try to scam you. Hopefully it's not much to fix."

"Thanks," I say, feeling better. "We're hoping to hit the road early this afternoon."

"You're not staying the night?" he asks, seeming puzzled, his eyes darting between Lucas and me.

"Oh no, we're—we're just here on business. Unfortunately."

He looks slightly disappointed. "Oh. You guys still want to hand me your V cards?" he asks casually.

I nearly spit out my Arnold Palmer.

"Sorry-what, dude?" After everything Lucas has done in the past hour, this taking charge of things is agreeing more and more with parts of me that are typically asleep.

Justin looks puzzled. "Oh. You're not here for Valentine's Day," he states.

It's Lucas's turn to be puzzled. "Is it...? No, we're not."

Justin chuckles. "Sorry, guys. We have a Valentine's day festival here, and people get cards that get stamped, and if your card is full, you get rewards."

I giggle uncontrollably when he leaves.

Lucas gives me a crooked half smile and digs into his dish. "Admit it."

"What?"

"You were hoping for it."

"Whaaaat? That is so...wrong on so many levels."

He takes a long draw on his beer. "Name one."

For starters, I'm not a virgin. But of course, *he'd* think I'm a virgin. "Well," I say. But my brain stays stuck on that tidbit of misinformation, and I'm unable to proceed any further.

Justin comes back right on time and hands us each a card.

Emerald Creek Valentine's Festival Punch Card

"We just call 'em V cards here. I see how that could be confusing. I punched where it says O*rder The Same Food*. Just being thorough. Thought you might be curious." He leaves us to take care of other customers.

"He's not my type," I say too quickly after he leaves.

"You have a type?"

"Everyone has a type."

"I don't."

I almost choke on my food. Now that the work part of this trip is over, I'm more relaxed. I feel like messing with him. Back to what he just said, I guess it could be argued he has lots of types. But there's a common thread. "You know bimbos are a type, right."

"Bimbos? That's my type?"

"Well, duh." I shoot him a teasing grin, but the unpleasant tingle of jealousy tugs at me.

This isn't me.

And yet when his phone rings, and I snatch it from the table, turning the screen toward him. *Bimbo,* I mouth silently as I shove the picture of a cute blonde smiling at him from the screen. *BabyM* is the name under the picture. Yuck.

He takes the phone from me and walks away from the table so I can't hear his conversation.

I look at the card, and I have to say, it's a cute idea. There are categories like Self Care (Get A Massage / Get My Hair Done/ Get A Manicure), Get A Meaningful Gift For My Loved One (Flowers / Chocolates / Perfume / Other), Do Something Sweet For My Loved One (Give Them A Foot Massage / Clean Their Car / Other), Share A Secret With My Loved One (*Self-Stamp*).

Justin indeed punched our V cards where it says, Share A Dish With My Loved One.

"Where are you taking her?" I ask as Lucas returns to the table.

"What? Who?"

"Your girlfriend. Where are you taking her tonight?"

He cocks his head to the side and squints his eyes. "I haven't decided yet." I know he's thinking about the girl on the phone but *god*—can you imagine if that sexy dreamy look on his face was for me? Heat creeps from my middle to my chest, up my neck, and to my cheeks, just fantasizing about that.

Right.

Like that's ever going to happen.

I shake myself out of my self-induced misery. "Should we check on the car?" It's almost one o'clock. It should be ready.

It has to be.

Chapter Four

Lucas

"Fuck." The car's suspension is toast, and the subframe is bent. Colton doesn't have the parts. Thalia doesn't have Triple-A and neither do I. We can't get a rental until tomorrow.

We're stuck here.

At least my uncle was cool on the phone. "Just do what you need to do," he said.

I'm texting Mads.

She's having another good day. No pain. No anxiety—not even when I tell her I won't make it back before tomorrow. I'm the one who's panicking. She texts something about the universe having my back.

She's constantly telling me to go out with girls. That I'm wasting away because of her. One day she even said I was her third victim, and that nearly killed me. I might have told her about Thalia then. She might have helped me come up with this trip idea.

I'm lying. She totally engineered that one.

Thalia's cool reaction (*"It'll give me the opportunity to learn more about the town"*) is just a front. The red blotches on her neck tell a different story each time she hangs up from trying to find us a place to stay.

The resort was the obvious go-to, but they're packed solid with the festival.

Same with the smaller hotel in town.

The Airbnbs have been sold out for weeks.

"There's a bed-and-breakfast you could try," Justin says.

Ten minutes later, we're at the entrance of a cape house on a side street sloping down to the lake.

"We're looking for two rooms," I say.

"You're in luck," the woman, who introduced herself as Miss Angela, says while she grabs two keys. "I had a cancellation. Follow me."

We go up a creaking staircase and down a short hallway decorated with naive paintings. There's only one door.

"Oh, it's adorable!" Thalia exclaims. The wood-paneled room is small, decorated like a log cabin, with twinkling lights above the massive bed, a rocking chair, and a tiny reading nook under the single window overlooking the snowed-in landscape. "I'll take this one," she declares.

Miss Angela hands us each a key. "Well then, it's settled."

"Where—where's my room?" I ask, following her outside.

"Your room?" She points to the room where Thalia is standing, looking outside the window, all traces of stress suddenly dissipated from her shoulders. "That's the only room I have."

Thalia turns around, her eyes like saucers.

"Gotcha," I say.

"What?" Thalia squeals, like she doesn't understand.

But the only answer she gets is the sound of Miss Angela's light footsteps down the stairs.

"I'll take the..." The options are the rocking chair or the reading nook. "I'll sleep on the floor," I say. There's a thick carpet on the antique pine floorboard. It could be worse.

Thalia looks dejected as she plops on the bed. "That sucks." She toys with her phone, as if another option will suddenly present itself.

As if we hadn't wasted the last hour calling every place in a thirty-mile radius.

Not that we would even have a vehicle to get us thirty miles from here.

"It's no big deal," I say.

She sighs. "I should type up my report."

Chapter Five

Thalia

"You need to loosen up. Carly can wait."

I glance up at Lucas. Earlier he walked to the general store to get us necessities while I got some work done. Then we took turns taking a quick shower. Now I'm plopped on the super comfy king size bed, typing like crazy on my laptop. He's in the rocking chair, swinging back and forth, folding the V card brochure in the shape of a fan. He's very distracting, and I'm not talking about his constant movement. "It's Carla," I say and go back to typing my report.

"This town is cute. Totally your style. We should visit it."

I've been dying to. It's got a bunch of different architecture styles—federalist, colonial, Greek revival, postmodern, rehabbed barns and more—two covered bridges as far as I could see, and too many cute shops for a small town in the middle of nowhere.

It's my dream come true.

"I'll get to it," I answer. He's appointed himself as my assistant, and I can see how he'll want to follow me everywhere.

Not doing that.

"Let's go," he says.

"You can go. I'm good."

"What's wrong?"

I roll my eyes. "Did you not see the hordes of couples?"

"*Hordes* of couples?" He repeats, frowning. "Yeah. The guy said it was Valentine's Day or some shit. What's wrong with that?"

Valentine's Day or some shit? Wow. Suddenly I feel compassion for the bimbo on his phone. That can't be fun.

"Valentine's Day is the single person's punishment," I inform him.

His frown deepens. "Really."

"Really. You wouldn't know, you probably haven't considered yourself single since you were...what—twelve years old?"

His frown breaks, and what sounds like a sincere laugh fills the room. He stands, dwarfing the bedroom.

"Come on, Tally, forget the computer. Let's paint this town pink," he says in a cheery voice, tapping on the V card list of things to do on Valentine's Day.

He can't be seriously considering doing this. "It's Thalia."

His smile turns from surface level happy to deep and tender. "I know it's Thalia," he says in a softer voice. "It means to flourish."

What is he *doing?*

"Don't do that," I say, pretending to focus on my computer when my insides are turning to mush. All this because a hot guy is paying me some attention. How pathetic of me.

"Do what? I'm looking after you. You're wilting in a hotel room instead of flourishing."

It's an adorable bed-and-breakfast room, but yes, I do feel like I'm wilting when there's so much beauty outside. "You're pretending to flirt," I snap back.

He grunts but doesn't deny it. Thalia 1, Lucas 0.

"It's going to get dark pretty soon, and you won't be able to see all those pretty houses," he insists.

I sigh and give in to that argument. Thalia 1, Lucas 1.

It's worse than I expected. There are *throngs* of couples lovingly strolling the streets, holding hands, sharing hot chocolates, going in and out of shops. That's exactly the type of situation I actively avoid.

I can't be partaking in this with Lucas Hunt by my side. I'm awkwardly avoiding contact with his body, but the narrow sidewalk pushes us together each time we cross a couple. At one point, after I've taken numerous photos of the public library, a pink sandstone and limestone building in a stunning Romanesque style, he hooks his strong arm around my shoulders briefly to guide me around a snowbank.

That's it.

I've reached my limit. We are way too down my personal fantasy lane for safety.

"If we get this card punched," he says, "we get free drinks at tonight's karaoke at Lazy's. I say we can do it."

I grimace. Free drinks and karaoke on Valentine's Day? A recipe for disaster. "Hard pass."

"I knew it," he says. "You're too chicken."

I thought he was going to call me boring. "Chicken for what?"

"Well, obviously, the karaoke. But also, all this other shit."

I glance at the sheet. "I'm just not interested."

"Uh-uh. You're scared."

Scared? Has he met me? I turn my eyes to him. "Nothing scares me, Hunt. I just happen to have different life goals than yours."

"Are you sure?" There's defiance in his smirk.

"Pff. Yyyeah." Lucas Hunt is the boss's nephew. Rumor has it he'd be a great worker if he didn't call out so often. So yeah, I know we have different life goals. We have different life challenges.

"Here's what I think. I think you're scared of pushing your boundaries. Of coloring outside the lines. Of crossing—"

"I get your metaphors. Were you listening this morning? Or just texting the entire time."

He flinches. "My point exactly. Except at work. And that's how you excel. If only you'd let that spark spread to your personal life, you'd be on fire."

My jaw drops at his words. Should I be offended? Or was that a compliment?

"I don't even know how to answer that," I say.

"I can't blame you," he has the nerve to say. "Back to your life goals. I hear you. You're putting your career first. Well, *this* is your opportunity to secure the contract," he says, flicking his nail on the brochure.

So much bullshit, I just shake my head.

"This town is run by a Select Board that decides on local regulations and approves all permits," he continues. This isn't news to me. Even if the resort chooses my project for their renovations, nothing will be final, and the work won't start until we've secured the necessary authorizations. "There's a significant overlap between the people who'll approve your project, and the businesses who organize this...thing. Might be time for you to do some schmoozing."

"That's...unethical."

"Getting to know people is not unethical. You're just scared," he says, pointing to my chest.

"I am not scared of anything."

"Not even of jumping cows?" He chuckles.

"It was huge!"

A half hour later, I'm in a Georgian house right off The Green. More specifically, in the beauty salon occupying its first floor. I would have happily spent more time photographing the dentil molding and taking measurements of the floor plan, but I'm here to prove a point.

That I'm not a chicken.

So I'm receiving a shoulder massage while my face mask does what it's supposed to do and my feet rest on a heating massage pad.

Proving my bravery to Lucas has its upsides.

Earlier, the spa owner, Grace, lit candles, put music on, and served me herbal tea in a hand-thrown pottery mug. "I hope you don't mind, but my friends want to drop by and say hello," she says.

Um—sure?

Grace is about my age. She has a lush mane of black curls, and a sunny smile she dispenses generously. "We have a private social media here, called Echoes. That's how they know about you."

"That's..." I don't know how to say this.

"Sounds a bit creepy, I know," Grace smiles. "Until it comes handy. Like if say, you're stranded with a totaled car on one of the busiest days of the year and you desperately need a room. Or a mechanic. It's really harmless. People looking out for each other."

So that's how everything got sorted out so quickly? Interesting.

I'm thinking about the charm of small-town living when I hear, "You're Daisy's victim!" My eyes plop open and focus on a woman about my age taking off her coat. She flashes a dimpled smile and hands me a heart-shaped cupcake with pink and red sprinkles. "I'm Alex. I thought you'd need some comfort food."

The face mask stretches my skin as I take a bite of the cupcake and immediately moan.

"Nothing like local, small batch," Alex says as a way of explaining the deliciousness that just hit my palate. She sets a whole tray of cupcakes on a side table.

"Who's Daisy?" I ask.

"The Kings' Angus. She resents their Jerseys," Grace says. "Close your eyes, honey. Serum coming in."

What on earth is she talking about? I close my eyes.

"Daisy's the cow," Alex explains, then sighs. "Man, this festival is exhausting. If another couple hands me their phone to take a photo of them in front of the covered bridge, I might legit puke."

I grin. "I feel your pain."

"That doesn't include you guys, Thalia. You guys are cute," Alex quickly adds.

"Oh, we're not a couple."

"Really?"

"Nope."

"I told you he's her colleague," another voice says. "You're his boss, right?" I lift one eyelid and see a redhead plopped on a foot stool two feet from me. "I heard the resort loooooved your concept. I'm Autumn. I'm a decorator."

"I must have missed a post on Echoes," Alex continues, "because the way he carried you out of the car and took care of you earlier was *waaay hot*."

Um...okay.

We're technically in a private treatment room, but it looks like half the town is gathering here instead of in the front room.

At least Grace's girlfriends are.

I don't mind in the least. I haven't been out with girlfriends since…let's see. Not counting going out to an arcade with my sister, her friends, and their kids, that would be…since I started working? Wow.

Autumn pops another cupcake in her mouth. "I like your ftuff the beft," she says with her mouth full. "I hope you get the contract."

"You two clearly have couple potential," Alex continues on her track.

"And how would you know that, Alex?" Grace says, removing my mask.

"Did you *see* how he *looks at her*?"

Grace laughs. "Oh yeah. Exactly like Chris looks at you."

Alex turns bright red and stands up. "Who wants a drink? I'm having some of Haley's bubbly."

"Who *doesn't* want Haley's bubbly?" Grace answers. "Autumn, honey, glasses are in this cupboard there. You're going to karaoke tonight, right Alex?"

"Maybe."

"Um—no," Grace says. "You're going. We're *all* going. And you too," she tells me. "It's the best place to be on Valentine's Day. And you're going to look gorgeous."

Another young woman joins the group and moves me to and from the hair wash station. Cupcakes are passed again. At some point, I end up with a glass of Haley's bubbly in my hand while Grace does my pedicure and the other young woman blow dries my hair, until Grace decides it's time for my manicure and Alex plops a straw in my glass.

The bottom line is, it feels like a beehive and I'm the queen.

I don't normally treat myself to lavish things like mani-pedis and blow dries, unless I'm going to a wedding. I certainly never had a massage. I can afford it now, but it still feels wasteful. Of money and of time.

But not today. Today it feels like a necessary indulgence.

Today I feel like I'm in a time and space warp where different rules apply.

"Holy shit," Alex says. The other women take a step back and look at me in awe. I turn to a mirror and...oh.

Wow.

I never knew my hair could be so lush and shiny. It falls in natural waves on my shoulders, framing my face, giving me a sexy edge that surprises me.

My heartbeat picks up as I take in the new me looking back in the mirror, and warmth spreads inside me. My skin seems to glow from the inside. Grace applied makeup after the facial, something natural like I asked. My eyes are discreetly smoky, making my gaze sensual. My lips capture the light with their nude lip gloss. And my cheekbones! I never noticed my cheekbones before.

My nails are a deep valentine red. I didn't have a say in that. The girls wouldn't have it any other way. I agree with them. And that seductive, go-getter color agrees with me. This is also who I am, deep inside.

A slow smile spreads on my face as I admire myself in the mirror. So this is how it feels to look hot.

I like it. I like it very much. I like it so much my eyes mist.

Total confidence boost.

So when Lucas texts me, *Ready for karaoke?*

You bet I am.

Chapter Six

Thalia

Lucas is standing in the middle of the bedroom when I get back to the bed-and-breakfast. A couple of bags are strewn on the bed, and there's a single rose on a pillow. My brain does a double take on the meaning of that, but then he swallows with difficulty and says, "Damn, Thalia. What are you trying to prove?"

Shit. She went too hard on the makeup. *I knew it.* This isn't for me.

I rush to the bathroom and grab the small black washcloth stitched, *Makeup.*

Lucas materializes behind me, our eyes locking in the mirror. "What the fuck?"

"Forget it," I mumble, bringing the damp cloth to my eyes.

His hand clasps my wrist. "What. Are. You. Doing."

"This isn't me. I'm washing it off."

"What do you mean, this isn't you?"

"It's...too sexy."

His grip relaxes around my wrist while his body molds against my back. "Damn right you're sexy. Get used to it." His voice rolls out like thunder, and electricity runs through me.

Our gazes are still locked. He's so close, I can feel his heartbeat. He runs his hand up to my throat, then down my blouse, unbuttoning it. "What are you doing?" I whisper. I have a severe case of melting panties. He needs to stop right away, but I can't find the words or the body language to impart that information to him.

I'm in Lucas overdrive, and I can't think straight.

When the two top buttons are undone, he moves to my sleeves and rolls them up, one after the other, slowly, trailing his rough fingers on my forearms.

"There," he says. "All set."

Then he turns me around, his hand on my hips, and takes a step back. "Damn, Thalia," he says again, his gaze spreading fire through my body. "I like what this town is doing to you."

He takes my hand and drags me out of the bathroom. "What's all this?" I ask. I need to regain control of the situation.

Do I like what he's doing to me?

Yes, I do. Too much. I like what he sees when he looks at me. I like that he's still holding my hand. I'm totally out of practice. I'm not used to this. He's just fooling around, even though he shouldn't.

I know better than that. I need to remind him of the girl on the phone. Hence, *What's all this*? There's a rose and a purple bag that says *Cassandra's Lingerie*.

He went shopping for his girl. He can't be flirting with another.

He drags the back of his finger across his eyebrow. "I...it's for the V card. I did some schmoozing. I'll tell you all about it at the pub."

He's not really flirting with me, is he? It's just that I'm not used to guys giving me compliments.

I need him to not be flirting with me. He has a *girlfriend*! He calls her Baby M. I need some faith in the male species. I've begun to really like Lucas Hunt. Please let him be a good guy.

Lazy's is packed, standing room only. The space is turned mainly into a dance floor, with a small stage against the back wall, high tables on the sides, candles flickering everywhere, couples holding hands, groups of friends chatting and laughing. Lucas got us two glasses of water, a beer for him and "something with an umbrella for you."

I had to laugh at that. "Is that what you ordered?"

"Nah. Justin said you'd had some local bubbly this afternoon, and that drink is based on it."

Well, looks like Echoes was active today.

Lucas tilts his beer bottle toward me to clink. Thirsty, I grab my glass of water and angle it toward him.

He pulls his beer bottle back. "Tt-tt. What are you doing?"

"I'm clinking! Happy Whatever!" Truth is, I *am* happy. There's a great vibe going on at Lazy's, lots of singles here tonight, including the group of young women who were at the salon. I don't feel awkward. The music is great. And it's good to feel sexy. It helps to be with a guy like Lucas. I've noticed a lot of girls—and guys—looking at us.

"You don't clink with a non-alcoholic beverage, Thalia."

"Says who? And why not?"

"Says the French. Seven years of bad sex."

I round my eyes at him and take a long gulp of water. "Well, *we're* not having sex *together*," I say in a low voice, "so..."

He narrows his eyes at me. "Doesn't matter. Grab your umbrella drink and clink like a big girl."

Our glasses are nearly empty when Lucas pulls the V card from his chest pocket.

"So, looks like we pretty much nailed everything on the card, except sharing a secret. You wanna start?"

I peek over. "It says *with my loved one.* '*Share a secret with my loved one.*'"

He narrows his eyes at me. "Work with me, Williams. I'm trying to save the firm some money. We're one punch from a free drink."

"Save the firm some money?"

He shrugs. "Yeah. Don't worry, I ran it by my uncle. There's no reason we should be out of pocket for this forced stayover."

"But...drinks?"

"Relax, it's nothing. And he gets the whole schmoozing thing too, so I went ahead and put your little...makeover on the company card." His eyes dance across my body.

"You *what*?"

"It's cool," he says, placing his hand on mine. He has large, calloused hands, warm and confident. He gives me a quick squeeze, and then his thumb rubs the inside of my wrist. He builds houses from the ground up with these hands. If he says it's cool, it's gotta be cool, right?

"Kay," I say, missing his hand as it leaves mine. "It still feel we're doing your girlfriend wrong, is all," I add. He needs to be set straight. Even if he's just a good guy looking out for me, even if the effect he has on me is unintentional on his part, what he's doing to my belly and parts south is very, very wrong by that poor girl.

"My girlfriend?"

Oh Lucas, don't do that. I sigh. "The bimbo on the phone? She's very cute, by the way. I didn't mean bimbo in a bad way." Suddenly, I don't want him to think I'm judging his girlfriend. He's been nothing but nice to me—it's only my fault I'm madly crushing on him—and I want us to be friends after this. "And I'm sure she's a great girl. I mean, she's your girlfriend, so..." I roll my eyes like this is the ultimate argument and finally shut my mouth.

"The bimbo on the phone?" He repeats, then takes his phone out and brings up the photo, a slow grin spreading on his face, love all over it. "Yeah, she's a great girl." The pad of his thumb strokes the surface of his phone.

Okay, there's no need to go this far. I mean, really. I'm having an out-of-body experience in this perfect place, with a perfect makeover, can I please continue to pretend I'm on a date with this perfect guy? There's no need to rub it in, Lucas.

"That's Madison." He pockets his phone and adds, "My little sister."

Oh. "Oh."

He smirks. "You didn't really think she was my girlfriend."

"I did!"

"Jesus, Thalia. What kind of guy goes for drinks with a hot colleague all dolled up on Valentine's Day if he has a girlfriend sitting at home?"

Wow. *A hot colleague.* Okay.

Then he continues, his voice a barely audible low rumble, "Especially if he's going to be sharing a bedroom with said colleague in a couple of hours."

Oh-oh. My jaw drops while I rack my brain for a witty comeback. Something a responsible colleague would say. I take a shallow breath, hoping the oxygen will help, start saying, "Well—"

His hooded eyelids shut me up.

I take a deep breath. I'm not sure I'm ready with where we're going here. Over the moon? Yes. Ready? No. Heat creeps again, from my middle to my cleavage to my neck and all the way up to my hairline.

"Ready?" he asks, pointing to the last line on the Valentine's punch card.

Moving on. "Sure."

"Ladies first. Tell me a secret."

I only have to think for a second. "I want to have my own architecture firm some day." That's a brash thing to say to the nephew of my current employer.

"That's not a secret."

"Yeah it is."

"Anyone who knows you can see that."

Really? "Oh." That's disappointing.

"Tell me something personal," he pushes.

Ugh. I look down my empty glass. "My older sister calls me Thamazon because she thinks I scare men away."

He laughs. "I like it. She's right. You *are* pretty scary." He signals Justin for another round. "Just one sister?" he asks.

I nod. "Older sister, married, two kids. My parents' pride and joy."

He tilts his head. "There's no way they're not proud of you too."

Are they, though? "Maybe. But mostly, they're worried."

We clink again with our freshly refilled drinks. "About what?" he asks, his gaze intently boring into mine.

The fuzzy drink hits my palate in a sweet explosion of bubbles. "They don't really understand why I'm so driven at work." I look away from him. I never talk about my relationship with my family. "They're very traditional. Blue collar. Hard working. But in their mind, the man should provide. In their mind, I'm too successful for my own good. That's what scares them."

"Do you show them what you do? Your designs? The buildings you've contributed to?"

I did, once. "It's best they don't know. They can keep pretending I'll eventually settle for a good man who'll take care of me."

Lucas grunts. "They should be proud of you."

"I prefer them happy."

"Whatever you say, Thamazon."

I swat his arm lightly. "*That*'s a secret. You can't repeat it." I hope he won't be going around the office calling me that, now. "Oh, look," I say, trying to erase my nickname from his memory, "those girls over there were all at the salon. That one is Grace, the owner of the salon, and the one who just sang is Alex."

"She seems like she had too much to drink," Lucas observes.

She does.

"The guy taking her home doesn't look too happy."

We crane our necks and watch as a tall guy pulls Alex to the door and helps her into her boots and coat, then takes her hand and crosses The Green holding her pumps in his other hand. She's straggling, holding him back. Until he hoists her on his shoulder.

"That should do it," Justin's voice comes from behind us. "They've been dancing around each other long enough."

The guy and Alex enter a Victorian house, then Lucas turns to me. "I have a follow-up question."

I frown. "That's not the game. You tell me your secret first, and we'll see about your follow-up question."

"Okay. When I was twenty-one, I became the legal guardian for Madison."

"Your sister?" I gasp. "What? How? Why?"

He chuckles. "That's three follow-up questions."

"Oh come on. You can't drop a bomb like that and not tell me more." The moment these words pass my mouth, I regret them. I'm being insensitive. There's no good way to become your sibling's guardian.

"I'll tell you more. Just answer my question first. When was your last boyfriend, and how long did it last?"

"College. Three months. That was two questions, by the way."

"College? That's...ages ago."

"Thank you, I'm not that old, but yeah. I guess my sister is right. I *do* scare men away. Am I scary?"

"That's a fourth question, Williams. Which one should I answer?"

I want to know about him, but I'm afraid I'll be probing too much. Now that I've had a couple of seconds to digest the fact that he's his sister's guardian, I realize my questions are not respectful. I raise my eyes at him but can't get the words out.

He smiles softly at me. "My parents died in a car accident when Mads was sixteen. That's how I became her legal guardian."

The music and voices around us seem to shut off, and it's like there's only him and me in that pub, and the world just tilted slightly on its axis. Nothing is what I thought it was. Lucas might be a golden boy, but he's had it way harder than I ever did. Heck, for all I know, there's nothing golden about him except his looks and his personality. "Oh no. Lucas."

His head hangs down, lost in memory. "She was badly injured in the crash, but she's doing much better now. You can't tell, if you don't know about it. At least physically, she's mended." He looks up toward me, and it's a shattered, complex man I'm staring at. "She still needs a lot of...help, though."

"That's terrible. Not about you looking after your sister, but losing your parents. And Madison being injured." Tears prickle my eyes. "I had no idea. I'm so sorry."

"That's why it's called a secret." He takes a swig of his beer. "Come on, let's dance."

"Are you sure?"

"One thing this has taught me, is to live my life to the fullest. So I'm here in this awesome bar, stranded with a beautiful woman, and the DJ knows what she's doing...hell yeah, I'm taking you on the dance floor."

My stomach does butterflies at his words. At his positivity. I stand next to him and naturally slide my hand in his as we walk to the dance floor.

"Give it up for Lucas and Thaliaaaaaa!" We both spin toward the DJ. But it's Grace holding the karaoke mic over the crowd like this is some rock concert. Cheers and applause surround us. "Come on up, guys!"

Lucas gives my hand a quick squeeze and bends over to talk in my ear. "You good with this? Karaoke?"

Do we have a choice? I shrug and laugh and squeeze his hand back.

A large grin spreads on his face. He pulls me up to the small stage. "Elton John, 'Your Song,'" he tells the DJ.

Cool. I know that one, right? Everybody knows that song.

But the lyrics start scrolling on the monitor, and Lucas's eyes bore into mine, and my eyes water. I wasn't prepared for that. I take a deep breath and look at the crowd instead. *Focus on the lyrics, Thalia.* Focus on the fact that even if Lucas is singing the words as if he'd written them for me, he didn't. He's not a songwriter. He builds houses.

And so do I.

And then.

Then.

We both mess up the lyrics. We look at each other and sing, *this house is for you.*

Lucas smiles, drops his head, grabs the mic, pulls me into his side, and we keep singing together, but looking at the audience this time. They're all singing with us, and we're carried by their energy, and thank god for that and for Lucas's arm around my shoulder because my legs aren't doing much carrying anymore.

Of course, Lucas's arm has a lot to do with that.

As we leave the stage, the DJ plays another slow dance, no karaoke this time, and Lucas lets out a low, satisfied growl. "About time."

With one hand between my shoulder blades and the other cupping my hip, sliding toward my lower back, he leaves me no choice but to twine my hands behind his neck and lay my head on his chest.

And then I feel his breath in my hair.

Chapter Seven

Thalia

We don't kiss, not in the pub.

And not when we get back to the room either.

"You should use the bathroom first," Lucas says while I take my boots off and leave them next to the door.

"You go ahead," I answer. "I take forever."

He grabs the paper bag he brought back from the general store and dumps the contents on the bed. Toothbrushes, toothpaste, cotton disks, face lotion, a vanilla and rose deodorant and a musk deodorant. A hairbrush and a comb. Q-tips. A small box he promptly shoves into his pocket.

Wow. "You thought of everything."

He shrugs and takes what he needs.

"Thanks for doing this," I say.

He hands me the purple bag that's on the bed and says, "This is yours."

The store logo says *Lingerie*. Ever since he's told me he has no girlfriend, I've been thinking. Who did he buy this for? It could have been for Madison. Or..."What do you mean?" I want him to say it. There's also the matter of the rose on the pillow.

"I got it for you. Earlier. Since you know...you didn't pack an overnight bag."

"You got me lingerie?"

He blushes slightly. "Sleepwear."

"And a rose?"

"I might have gotten carried away by the Valentine's Day atmosphere," he says sheepishly. God, he's so handsome.

He goes into the bathroom, and I start tidying the room.

Why is he so shy all of a sudden? Since he told me about his parents and Madison, it's almost as if he's a different person. A wall went down, but the cocky, flirty guy is gone.

Although the way he danced with me?

So hot.

There's no way he doesn't want more with me.

Am I scaring him?

I smell the rose and set it on a nightstand. I hang the bag from the General Store on the bathroom doorknob. The last item on the bed is the purple lingerie bag. I hesitate, then open it.

The sleepwear is a deep red slip-on with lace. I've never worn anything so sexy. If this is what he wants me to wear tonight...

He comes out of the bathroom wearing just boxer shorts, and my eyes zoom in on his body, built by years of working construction. I lick my lips and struggle to lift my gaze to his face.

"All yours," he says.

But he's several steps away from me already, setting his clothes on the rocking chair, spreading the extra blanket on the floor.

He's talking about the bathroom. So I grab the sexy nightie and take my turn. I spread the toothpaste he bought on the toothbrush he bought and brush my teeth. I run the comb he bought in my hair. I use the lotion he bought and the black makeup washcloth to remove the makeup he'd said he liked.

When I get back into the room, he's lying on the floor on his side, his back to me, lights dimmed, blanket up to his shoulders.

I stop in my tracks, feeling silly in my sexy lingerie.

I hop in bed and angrily pull the covers over me, turning my back to him, as if this makes any difference.

The hell with this. What did I do wrong now? What did I do to scare him?

Less than ten minutes go by. "Lucas," I say.

He groans.

"This bed is huge. There's no point in you sleeping on the floor. It's ridiculous. We can create a wall of pillows."

"I'm not sleeping in that bed with you, Thalia."

I flip on my back. "Why not? We're both adults."

He grumbles, something that sounds like, "Exactly."

Great. "What are you scared of?" I ask him.

He never answers.

His breathing is irregular. The blanket rustles with each of his movements.

Through the small window above him, the full moon stares at us.

What kind of guy goes for drinks with a hot colleague all dolled up on Valentine's Day if he has a girlfriend sitting at home?...Especially if he's going to be sharing a bedroom with said colleague in a couple of hours."

There's no way he's not thinking what I'm thinking. Did he change his mind about me?

"I'm here in this awesome bar, stranded with a beautiful woman, and the DJ knows what she's doing...hell yeah, I'm going to take you on the dance floor."

What happened?

"You are pretty scary."

My sister's right. I did something to scare him off. What was it? I rack my brain and come up empty.

He clears his throat. I can almost hear his eyelashes batting. He's just as awake as I am. I prop myself on my elbow, looking down at where he's lying.

"Lucas!" I whisper-shout.

He turns on his back, one hand under his head. His bare chest, glistening in the moonlight, heaves with his breaths.

I wet my lips.

As my eyes glide down his body, my middle heats up.

"Are you sleeping?" I ask again, careful to bring my eyes back to his face.

He groans.

I sit on the bed and swing my feet to the floor.

His eyes fly open. "Stay in that bed, Thalia." His jaw clenches.

I slide to the floor and get to my knees, crawling the couple of feet that separate us. I place a hand on his hard chest. His heart is beating a million beats a minute.

So is mine.

I glide my hand down to the blanket, but he doesn't react. Should I...? I can't bring myself to.

I pull the blanket up to his chin. "You're going to get cold," I whisper.

What is he thinking?

Then I lean down as if to kiss him.

He stops me with a finger on my chin. "What are you doing?"

Good question.

"Thalia," he says, his thumb and forefinger holding my chin. "What do you want?" It's too dark for me to read the expression with his face turned to me, away from the moonlight.

I lick my lips. "I want to sleep with you." There's no way he doesn't know this. I'm throbbing and wet and desperate, and maybe he can't know this, but my nipples are pebbling through the thin fabric of the nightie he bought me, and there's no way he can't tell.

Plus, why would I be kneeling next to him? His question makes no sense.

He's a good guy, and he just wants to make sure we're on the same page. He doesn't want to take advantage of me. That has to be it, because I may not have had a boyfriend for years, but I'm not a nun, and I know that a man knows when I want him. There's generally no need to spell it out.

But Lucas makes no move to pull me against him. He lets go of my chin and stares out the window, looking hurt.

Shit. "I'm sorry." I scramble to my feet and turn around to jump back in bed.

His hand clasps my ankle. Then he's standing behind me, his front to my back, his erection pressed against my lower back, his hand wrapped around my waist.

"I don't want to just sleep with you, Thalia," he says. "You've been under my skin since I first met you, and if you're mine tonight, I want you mine for...a very long time." His finger trails the bare skin of my arm. "So if you're looking for a one-nighter, there's nothing wrong with that, but I'm not your man."

Lucas Hunt has had me under his skin *since he met me?* My knees weaken, and my head drops to his shoulder.

He continues. "I know how hard you fight for what you want, and I know the passion you put into your work. I know how fiercely you love your family, and I know how well you treat your coworkers. And I know the patience you have with your supervisor, because you probably think she has her reasons for being a bitch that have nothing to do with you." He dips his lips to the crease where my neck meets my shoulder. "You're wrong about that," he says against my skin, "but that makes you an even better person."

A zing goes straight down my center, touching my soul as it goes. "And going on that, I bet you're a fierce, loyal friend. And going on *that*, I'll bet you're an incredible lover. And I don't want to find out overnight that I'm right, only to lose you in the morning."

He lets go of my body, takes a step back, and I shiver in the sudden cold.

"I don't want to sleep with you, Thalia," he continues. "I want to *make love to you*. And I want to give you so much more than that. I don't want to be a notch on your bedpost. I want you to *know* me. So if this is not what you want, climb in bed, and we'll forget about this. But if you want me the way I want you, turn around, look me in the eyes, and tell me you'll be mine."

Chapter Eight

Thalia

A notch on *my* bedpost? Making *love* to me? Where is this all coming from?

My body takes over. The turning around, I can do, and I do it slowly, deliberately.

The looking in the eyes is harder, because he has me pinned somewhere between desire and commitment, and I'm afraid that once I drown in his eyes, I'll say yes to anything.

I can't make promises I won't hold.

What would it look like, to be with Lucas for *a very long time*? Why does he even want me that way? What does he see in me? Apart from all the...nice things he just said about my loyalty and having me under his skin.

Right now, my eyes are trained on his pecs. They're heaving slightly, his breath labored. I pinch my lips together and look up at his throat. His Adam's apple bobs. My gaze travels to his eyes. "I can't promise you forever, Lucas. We barely know each other. It'd be crazy."

He licks his lips, a quick swipe of the tongue, and his eyes sparkle. "Yeah, I'm a little crazy like that."

I drop my eyes. So this is it, I guess. I lean against the bed, ready to crawl up under the covers. I did what I could to get what I wanted, but I'm not going to lie to him.

"Give me three months," he says.

"Wh-three months?" My heartbeat picks up. Three months, I can do. Oh my god, three months sounds perfect. Okay then, can we both jump into bed now? "Why?" is my stupid ass answer.

He cocks his head to the side. "That's the longest you lasted. I like a challenge. Three months."

Three months with Lucas will be more intense, more demanding, and probably more exhausting than three months with my college boyfriend. Is this really what I want? Can I even afford a relationship right now, with everything going on at work? One night was so much more reasonable.

He leans over me, pushes the strap of my nightie off, and kisses my shoulder.

I take a sharp inhale. My nipples peak stronger through the satin fabric. I clench the comforter with both hands, or I might pull him to me. I haven't said yes to his offer yet.

He trails kisses from my shoulder up my neck. My head falls to the other side on its own, and I can't help the moan that escapes my lips.

"Was that a *no*?" he asks, his mouth against my jaw, peppering kisses up my ear. He cups my chin between two fingers.

"No, it wasn't," I breathe.

"You're going to have to be more specific, Thalia. I'm losing it here. I want to fuck you seven ways to Sunday for the next twelve weeks. I just need to know that you're on board. Like I said, I don't want to sample you. I know I'm going to need more than one night with you."

He's *losing it*. Gorgeous, cocky, athletic, Lucas Hunt says he's losing it because I haven't consented to sleeping with him for the next three months. To getting to know him for the next three months. Yet.

Meanwhile, I'm a hot mess down there. I don't know how long I can keep this going. "I thought you said you wanted to make love to me."

He growls and pulls the strap off the other shoulder. "That didn't seem to convince you. Look, when all is said and done, if you say the word, there'll be a lot of fucking and a lot of lovemaking. I guarantee it."

I'll give him that. The man knows how to talk to a woman. "Okay," I whisper. "Three months."

A slow grin spreads on his face. He lowers his lips to mine, barely grazing them at first, and I close my eyes. His breath is warm and sweet, with a trace of mint. He seals our mouths together, and his tongue starts a slow exploration, lapping inside me, almost tentative at first, until I meet his strokes with my tongue, and he invades me with a growl.

As if he was waiting for my permission.

His kiss is soft and strong, just like him, and it's profound too, and reverent, like a promise. And when his arms tighten around my whole body—god!

He breaks the kiss and says against my lips, "I knew you'd be sweet, baby, but fuck." He nips at my bottom lip. "Fuck!"

Three months. Three months of this. What have I done to deserve him?

My whole body thrumming, I fist his hair. "Lucas..."

"I got you, babe." He puts his arms around my waist and lifts me higher on the bed, then does quick work of my nightie. "God, Thalia, you're so beautiful. Knew you were beautiful under all those tight ass clothes."

Tight ass?

He chuckles as he kisses my collarbone, down between my breasts, then takes one nipple, sucking on it gently, then harder, until I arch under his pressure.

"That's it, babe. Right where I want you," he mumbles as he trails his strong, calloused hands up and down my body, as if he wanted everything at once. As if he didn't know where to start.

Am I a tight ass?

"Your clothes, babe. Not you," he grumbles, as he takes his time moving to my other nipple and starts torturing it equally, making me writhe under him.

"You're *hot.* Fucking hot."

Lucas Hunt thinks I'm effing hot.

My eyes flutter closed, then fly open when he moves down to my belly, kissing his way down to my center.

"Fucking clothes make you even hotter."

My legs drop open for him on a moan.

He groans as his tongue explores my folds, and *god*.

God!

He flicks and sucks and laps me, and when he runs his hands up to my breasts and lightly pinches my nipples, I come undone. He enters me with two fingers, his thumb stroking my clit.

And then our eyes connect, and there's awe in his.

How had I missed all the times he was, actually, looking at me? How had I discarded those as accidents?

I'm not a screamer, but here, in this bedroom, under Lucas Hunt's hands and mouth and his gaze, I come inside out and scream, abandoning myself to him.

And after he cups my center with his palm, collecting the last of my orgasm, he crawls to me, pulls me to his chest, and cradles me in his arms, drawing slow strokes on my naked back, kissing my hair while I catch my breath.

His erection strains his boxer shorts, his breathing is labored, his heartbeat bangs loudly against his chest, yet he's *letting me catch my breath*.

Three months of this?

God.

God! What have I done?

I run my hand down his beautiful, chiseled abs and under the thin fabric.

He lifts his hips. I get him totally naked, and my mouth waters at the sight of him. Long and thick, veined and beating for me. I stroke him, making him moan and making me wet again.

A drop of precum pearls, drawing me down. There's no resisting Lucas, in life or in bed. I lower my mouth to him and lick it off. *Oh god.* Just the smell of him makes me wet. What is happening to me?

He holds my hair back so he has a better view and says, "You don't have to, Thalia."

My belly clenches at his raw voice and his words. No, I don't have to. But I want to. And it's not because this beautiful alpha male is moaning and groaning for me under my hands and that's the sexiest thing that's ever happened to me. It's not because giving him pleasure alone might make me come.

It's because under all that gentleness, that care, that attentiveness lavished on me over the past day, there's a beast ready to take me on and turn my life upside down, and I *like* it.

I want it.

I might have been under his skin for a long time, but he just touched my heart.

"I want to," I murmur, my mouth already around him. I take him as deep as I can, slowly at first so I don't gag. He's so long, I wrap my hand at the base of his shaft and stroke him as I lick and suck him.

He hisses, "Fuck, Thalia, slow down," his fingers bunching my hair.

I pull out and look at him. "Am I hurting you?"

He frames my face in his hands and caresses my eyebrows with his thumbs. "You could never hurt me. You're perfect."

Warmth spreads through my body at his words. I've never felt so comfortable having sex. Smiling, I lower and take him again, my clit clenching when he pulses in my mouth. I suck him harder and get into a rhythm.

He hits the back of my throat, cupping his hips up to meet me. I'm ready for him to come in my mouth, but he bucks out of my mouth and pulls me up to him, kissing me strongly, our teeth and tongues clashing.

Then he flips me on my stomach and trails kisses on my back, all the way to my butt. I'm ready for him.

Wanting for him to take me.

He runs his fingers between my legs and growls. "You're drenched again, Thalia. Fuck."

I wiggle my ass and look back at him over my shoulder. He's on his knees, erect above me, stroking himself while looking at me, arousing me just by the sight of him. My breath catches and our eyes connect.

"Get on your knees and hold on to the headboard," he orders while he steps off the bed. Gone is gentle Lucas, and boy, do I like his evil twin. He grabs a condom from the box in his pant pocket and sheaths himself, standing next to the bed, his eyes on me. "Good girl," he says when I'm where he told me.

On my knees, up and holding to the headboard.

He gets behind me, his front to my back, my hands on the headboard. Cupping my waist with one muscular arm, he tilts my ass toward him and bothers my nipple with his free hand.

I moan. His dick beats against my entrance, and I writhe against him.

"You want this, don't you," he growls against my neck.

"God, yes, please, Lucas."

"Good girl. So polite." He thrusts inside me, and I scream.

He's. So. Big.

He pulls back out, and I whine. "Lucas, what—"

He thrusts back in.

I moan.

He feels. So. Good.

He pulls halfway out, massaging my insides with shallow movements, then pushes back in slowly.

"Oh my god, Lucas. You feel so good."

He growls. "That's my girl." He gets into a rhythm, short, tormenting strokes followed by a deep thrust. My back arches even more, my toes start tingling, and my head falls against the headboard. Stroke after stroke, he builds me up. "You like that, babe?"

My orgasm rolls out on a wail.

He pulls me away from the wall and onto him, pounding into me from behind, holding my limp body with his strong hands as he rides his own orgasm, clutching me tight against him.

Once he relaxes, he brings us down on the mattress, his massive body cupped around mine, his hand slowly stroking my arm.

I feel safe.

And for the first time in my sex life, I turn around in the arms of the man who's given me so much already. I nestle in his embrace.

I *cuddle*.

And he cuddles back.

At some point, he must have taken care of the condom, because it's gone. But he did it without leaving me. And he doesn't leave the bed to clean up.

I sink deeper into his arms.

"What?" he asks in a sleepy voice.

"We smell like sweat and sex. I like it."

I feel more than hear his chuckle. "Yeah. I like it too. Don't want to clean it off yet."

"No," I sigh.

He holds me tighter against him. "Besides, you're too comfy."

I swing my leg across his hips. "Mmm."

He's getting hard again.

Mmm.

I'm a little sore. My lady parts aren't accustomed to the lumberjack treatment they just received. They're not complaining, though. In fact, they're very much on board with what's going on between Lucas's legs.

I'm warm and tingling, and I rock my center against his hip to satisfy my need.

Lucas rubs his coarse chin against my hair, trails his hand down my sides, and gives my ass a squeeze. I lick his nipple in response. He reaches over to the condom box.

His kiss this time is deep and slow and tender. His hands explore me, caressing my hair, massaging my shoulders. His gaze never leaves mine as he sets me on my back, moves between my hips, and hitches my leg over his shoulder. He enters me slowly and powerfully, stretching me carefully. "This okay?" he asks.

Is it okay to be treated like a queen, revered, cared for, pleasured?

"God, Lucas, you have no idea." He smiles softly at this, his eyes deep into mine as he goes in and out of me, bringing me slowly to ecstasy once again, the unspoken feelings in his gaze just as powerful as his strokes.

When I start clenching around him, he cups my nape in his big hand, brings my forehead against his, and our breaths mingle, growing ragged. I nibble his lower lip. I want more of him. All of him. I'm totally wrapped around him, legs, arms, and core, and his name is on my lips in a soft wail as I explode and he falls apart inside me.

For a few beats we lay still, him slightly to my side so he doesn't crush me with his weight. Our hearts are beating like mad, but our breaths are shallow now.

It's as if we're holding it in, wondering what just happened.

Nothing happened, Thalia. You just had great sex, and you're going to have more of that. Just enjoy the moment.

I force a deep breath, my moment of uncertainty finally behind me. Nothing like a little self pep talk.

His arms tighten around my chest as he buries his head in my neck and suckles on my tender skin, tickling me.

I giggle. "Are you trying to give me a hickey?"

He growls. "Maybe. I want to mark you, Thalia. Three months, remember?" He looks at me, a boyish grin on his face.

I laugh. "We're not teenagers anymore, Lucas." I laugh even harder when he dips back to my neck and sucks again.

Chapter Nine

Thalia

My hand goes to that spot on my neck when Carla says, "How do you explain this?"

I haven't seen Lucas since we came back, and I'm relieved. This was a bad idea. On so many counts. For one, you don't date the boss's nephew. Everybody knows that. And second, nerdy girls don't sleep with hot lumberjacks. Everybody knows that too! Except this nerdy girl, apparently. What was I thinking? For example, I don't even know how to act around him should he show up at the office! Is he my *boyfriend*? Or did I only consent to casual sex for three months? Are we even exclusive? I have no idea.

That's how much out of my depth I am.

And there's more. I can't stop thinking about him. I'm like, borderline obsessed, reliving our day and our night and our drive back together. The things he said to me. The way he touched me.

The way he made love to me.

That's not normal, right? The way I think about him. It's not healthy.

I never, ever should have slept with Lucas Hunt.

Again—what was I thinking?

"What were you thinking?" Carla snaps.

I'm in her office. Heather from HR is there as well, so there's that.

And on her desk are the expense reports for the trip to Emerald Creek.

I can answer that. Lucas said his uncle was cool with that, right? And if he's not, or if Carla's not, I'll just refund the firm.

No biggie.

I clear my throat and point to the first slip. The lingerie. Let's get the most embarrassing out of the way.

"I'm going to spare us all some time," Carla says before I can open my mouth. "This is inappropriate conduct. We won't stand for it." She leans forward and whispers, pretending it's so Heather from HR can't hear, "That's one step removed from sexual harassment."

Now my mouth is open, and it stays that way. Sexual har—? What the hell is happening? So maybe I haven't seen Lucas since we came back—we've both been busy with work, and he's on a job outside the city. But we've been texting and talking daily, and he wants me to meet his sister this weekend.

He made plans for the three of us to go to the aquarium together. He even texted me the details last night! What is she talking about?

"Drinks, lingerie, a hotel room on the corporate card? You'll never be put in charge of a project again. I can guarantee you that. Not over my dead body. Lucky if you can find work."

Heather from HR sits taller in her chair, looking both a little nervous and more in control than Carla. "We don't want to make a thing out of it. We have a nondisclosure prepared. We'll retain these expenses on your last paycheck. If your future employers reach out to us, we'll simply say we parted amicably, but that you're not eligible for rehire."

Not eligible for rehire? My heart slams in my chest. That's a guarantee I won't get any good job elsewhere. Ever.

All because I gave into the temptation of Lucas Hunt.

I knew it. I knew all along I had to put my career first. I just didn't know how badly one mistake would affect it. It seemed so safe, in Emerald Creek. *He* seemed so safe. And he made *me* feel safe.

But I wasn't.

"Lucas said—" I start. Lucas said all the expenses were cool because we were schmoozing with Emerald Creek. Of course, that's not totally copacetic. If you're picky you might even call it bribery. But that would be pushing it. And that's not what she said. She called it inappropriate conduct.

Carla cuts me off. "Lucas Hunt was assigned to you as a mentee, and you took advantage of your position to have an inappropriate relationship with him."

Heather leans over. "One room, Ms. Williams. That's pretty damning."

"The town was packed, we were without a car, we were lucky to get the one room." I'm about to add that Lucas slept on the floor, but that wouldn't be true. I don't know what I'm dealing with here. My priority is my career, and right now it's jeopardized by a one-night stand.

"Are you denying there was an inappropriate relationship?" Carla says, not a question. Does she know? Ohmygod, did Lucas say something?

"Wait. Did Lucas file a complaint against me?" *You've been under my skin for a long time... Give me three months.* Did he play me? Does he think that because he's the boss's nephew, he can get away with anything? Did he joke at the water cooler about sleeping with the nerd? Am I so clueless I can't even tell when someone's taking me for a ride?

That's possible. Totally possible. Heat creeps up to my hairline.

Carla crosses her arms, a tight smile of victory stretching her lips. "So you're saying there was. It's against our corporate policies, as it should be. Add to that the fact that Lucas reported to you."

"Did Lucas file a complaint?" I repeat, needing to hear it.

"He doesn't need to," Heather says. "And I strongly advise you against reaching out to Lucas Hunt at this time and any time in the future. It would only make your situation worse. As your former employer, if you talk to

Lucas Hunt now, we'll have to press charges against you, regardless of how the victim feels about this."

The vic...? *The victim?*

Oh my god. I did. I totally did come onto him. I wanted to have sex with him. I propositioned him.

Well, but...he didn't sound pressured. At. All.

And he demanded—demanded!—three months with me.

You've been under my skin for a long time.

"Stay away from Lucas, Thalia, and we'll see what we can do about your references," Carla adds with a side glance to Heather.

It doesn't matter what he said or how he made me feel, back in Emerald Creek. The fact is, I just lost my job because of what we did there, and there's no way he doesn't know that.

He's the boss's nephew.

I spend the rest of Friday at home, too stunned to even cry, trying to deconstruct what might have happened with Lucas, and I come up empty.

Focus on your career, Thalia. It's the only thing that counts.

Yep, I always knew that, and the one time I make an exception, here's where it gets me. One slip, and I lost my job. Not just any job. This was the launch of my career. I was working my way up this midsize firm. Making a name for myself, project after project. Getting experience, garnering recognition.

I feel lost. What now? I don't even know where to start. And the worst part is, I can't stop thinking about Lucas.

I fall asleep on the couch and wake up midmorning on Saturday to a melted ice cream bin spilled on the floor and Netflix asking me if I'm still watching *New Girl*.

I tidy up the living room, get in the shower, change my sheets, do my laundry, then manically clean the fridge, vacuum and mop the whole place (it's not that big), and dust the shelves. Not just surface dusting. I pull every book and chachka out so there isn't the risk of a speck of dust left. When there's nothing left to clean, I scour the oven.

Early afternoon, Lucas texts me: *Where are you?* And my heart breaks. We were supposed to meet at the Aquarium. He must be there now, with his sister.

My thumb glides over my phone's screen.

There's no way he doesn't know what happened. Right? Then why is he doing this? He knows the consequences.

"Stay away from Lucas, Thalia, and we'll see what we can do about your references."

My phone rings, and just the sight of his name spears my heart.

What if he doesn't know? I should at least tell him why I can't see him anymore.

But then if he's the person I thought he was, he'll go straight to Carla and make a fuss. *"If you talk to Lucas Hunt now, we'll have to press charges against you."*

I lost Lucas, and I lost my job. I don't need to make this worse.

Eyes stinging, I block his name in my list of contacts.

Taking a shaky breath, I look out the window. I could use a run, work out the tension, but the sidewalks are covered in snow, and there are patches of ice on the road.

I pace around my apartment instead. Call a few friends. Everyone is busy, and you know what? I don't really care. I'll be shit company right now, and who needs that?

I don't understand the whole inappropriate conduct angle. If I could afford one, I'd get a lawyer, because that sounds like BS to me, but that's off the table. Next week I'll update my resume, contact my small network.

Right now, I can't do anything productive, apart from cleaning my place, and that's done.

So I go to my parents'.

I know. I'm regressing.

At least I'm aware of it. I accept it. Name it. Embrace it.

It's Saturday evening, and they're babysitting my nephews. They still live in the split ranch I grew up in. Not much has changed. Mom and Dad say they believe in traditions, when really, they're stuck in their ways, and that's alright. They're happy.

We watch cartoons, play Go Fish, and eat mac'n cheese.

"What's a pretty girl like you doing alone on a Saturday night?" Dad finally asks. He kept it in for most of the evening.

"At least she's not working," Mom sneers.

"By the way, how *is* work?" Dad asks.

"Oh no! We are *not* talking about her career. Her career is what is ruining her life. Can we just have a nice family dinner, talk about normal things?"

Spot on, Mom. Dad hands me another beer, I load my plate with a second serving of mac'n cheese, and we talk about normal things.

Chapter Ten

Lucas

"She stood me up. I can't fucking believe it."

"It happens, Luke," Mads says. "Lots of fish in the water. Pun not intended." We're at the entrance of aquarium, and Thalia is an hour late.

I try her phone once again, but it goes straight to voice mail. She might be out of battery, or out of network.

Shit.

"You're not actually worried, are you?" my sister asks.

"I don't know." We were so good. We've been texting back and forth ever since we came back from Emerald Creek, and we've talked each night before going to sleep.

Okay, not yesterday, but I didn't think much about it. Chalked it up to work.

She mentioned having a meeting with Carla first thing in the morning, and these always mean extra work or extra shit for her. It's not a secret at the firm that Carla has a bone to pick with Thalia, and that she works her super hard. I can't wait for her to change departments. "Maybe."

"Do you know where she lives?"

When we returned from Emerald Creek, I dropped her off. She lives in a one-bedroom apartment on the first floor of a three-story brick building, not in the best neighborhood, but it's affordable, and at least it's hers. Thalia values her independence. "Yeah, I know where she lives."

"Then let's go," Madison says. "So you can put it behind you. You're going to be worrying all weekend if you don't. I don't know if I'd rather deal with you worried or angry. At least this time it won't be about me," she offers as a consolation.

There's light in the two windows of her place. I pull up to the curb and keep the engine going. Thick bushes would make it hard to get close on foot, and I'm not planning on spying on her. Before long, her silhouette appears.

She's pacing. She could be talking on the phone. I don't see anyone else.

She's not in the hospital. Nothing physical happened to her. I debate going to her door.

"We should go," Madison says softly, her hand on mine. "Her loss."

"Yeah." It's mine, though. Thalia was everything I wanted in a woman, and she didn't give me a chance to show her how good I could be for her. I was arrogant in asking for three months of her time.

What was I thinking? She doesn't have space for me in her life.

By the time the weekend is over, I've forgiven her broken promise. I went about this the wrong way. I should have courted her, wooed her. A woman like Thalia deserves to be treated better than I treated her. She shouldn't be forced into a relationship in exchange for sex. Fuck, now that I'm thinking about this, what I did sounds really wrong, and I can almost see where she's coming from.

Almost.

She could have made up a bullshit excuse instead of standing me up. Especially knowing Mads was going to be there. That was a little rude on her part. I thought she was more of a straight shooter. Then again, maybe she wants me to work a little harder for her. Not take her for granted.

I can do that.

I'm looking forward to it.

We shared something that night, even she can't deny it. I'm getting us back on track.

Game on.

I stop at a coffee shop on my way to the firm. Monday mornings, we have meetings at the office to go over the work for that week. Most guys head straight to the job sites, but my uncle wants me to be management someday, so he insists I show my face around here. He doesn't have children—never could keep a wife around long enough to start a family—and I no longer have parents, so here you go.

I take a latte to Thalia's desk, only to find it empty. Cleaned of all her belongings.

"Hey, Lucas," Carla sing songs. "How ya doin'?"

"Hey. Did Thalia change offices?" Maybe she got that promotion already, and they moved her to a different floor? But Carla's already in the meeting room.

"Lucas, in my office," my uncle says after the meeting.

Thalia never showed. I'm still holding two coffees, one nearly empty, the other full and cold. I ditch both in the nearest trash can and follow him.

He takes his time sitting down. Looks at me, rubs his face, and finally says, "What the fuck were you thinking?"

"Sorry—what's this about?"

"This is about you fucking my employees."

Okay. "F...what?" I don't like the plural, and I don't like the F-word, not in that context. Not coming from him.

"Carla had to let her go, you know. We don't do that around here. Kills the work ethic."

"Let who...Thalia?" That can't be. She all but got us the Emerald Lake Resort contract. She's up for a promotion. "Carla *let Thalia go*?"

"Had to."

My heart beats frantically in my ribcage. "On what grounds?"

He looks at me quizzically. "She didn't tell you?"

"On what grounds?" I repeat, gritting my teeth.

My uncle leans back in his chair. "Son, I'd take it easy if I were you. You're lucky you're family. Like I said, we don't do that around here. Especially on my money."

Wait. Is this about the expenses? A couple hundred dollars for a contract that will run in the hundreds of thousands? And, I ran it by him. He knows it. He approved it. I don't have a paper trail, but he gave me his okay. I keep my voice steady when I explain again. "They have a Valentine's Day festival there. I bought shit to get us in the good graces of the powers that be up there, for when they look at the permits."

"You fucked her, didn't you?"

That's not a question I'm willing to answer without more context. Thalia was let go because of what happened in Emerald Creek. But what part of it? "We only shared a room because the whole fucking place was sold out!" They can't possibly be letting go Thalia over something so small. "As for the nature of the expenses, it was my decision. And I'm the one who wrecked the car. Didn't mean to, but I was driving."

"This trip was under Thalia William's responsibility. Someone has to pay, it's her." He stands and goes to the window, hands in his pockets. "Besides, you can't afford to lose this job, Lucas, and you know it." He got that right. Madison, being my dependent, gets the health insurance she really needs through my job, and my uncle won't fire me for dropping everything when Madison has a panic attack and needs me right away.

I can't imagine what our lives would be like if we didn't have the safety net my uncle provides. But, especially at times like this, it doesn't mean I'm happy about the situation.

Thalia needs her job too.

My uncle isn't done, and it gets worse. "Carla had accounting breathing down her neck about the expenses. Got her panties in a twist. Now, it doesn't help that Carla wants the position Thalia applied for. For the past month, all I hear about is Thalia this, Thalia that. I can't deal with these fucking cunts. One of them had to go."

Did he just call Thalia and Carla *fucking cunts?* Rage boils inside me, and I can barely contain it.

I'm this close from quitting. I hate myself for sitting here, saying nothing to this misogynistic pig. But what are my options? Walking home to Madison, telling her we don't have health insurance until I find another job, and good luck with her next panic attack because I won't be there to help her through it? Or waiting until she's fully healed to follow my own path?

Following my moral compass or wrecking my sister's chances of recovery?

I do the right thing by my sister, and I sit this battle out.

"She'll be alright, son. We gave her a nice package, and she already has a couple of interviews lined up. For all I know, she'll be better off somewhere else. She's going places, and she'll get there faster now."

At least she's taken care of. I still don't understand why she didn't come Saturday. Why she didn't call me Friday, to tell me. We would have bitched about the firm. We would have talked things through. Brainstormed together what her next steps should be. It doesn't change anything between us, does it? We had a good thing going.

At least I thought so.

The next day, I read an email announcing Carla's appointment to the position Thalia wanted. A lateral move for Carla that would have been a promotion for Thalia.

No mention of Thalia leaving the firm.

I'm still hurt she didn't reach out to me, but hey, I get it.

She didn't feel bound by the promise she made me, and who could blame her?

After all, my uncle did fire her. Even if her career won't be impacted, she probably doesn't want to see my face.

She only wanted one quick fuck with me anyway.

Chapter Eleven

Thalia

Two weeks later, I receive the oddest phone call. It's from a lady named Cassandra in Emerald Creek. Like, the lingerie shop.

The little town has been popping up in my mind constantly since the job debacle, and it always brings a warm feeling to my heart. Apart from the hot night I spent with Lucas, which, no surprise, I now have mixed feelings about, thoughts of the town have been my only source of comfort.

Alex, Grace, and Autumn kept in touch via text message, and I've told them I lost my job. They were pissed I wasn't going to do the resort renovations—especially

Autumn—but Grace invited me to come stay with her anytime I wanted.

Alex sent a picture of Daisy trotting down Main Street.

The memories keep flowing.

Lunch over homemade beef brisket in front of a roaring fire to make up for the scare of Daisy the cow resulting in the car being as good as totaled.

Karaoke and singing and dancing with Lucas. Okay, scrap that memory. Karaoke and Alex being literally whisked away by her hunk of a man, the baker she works with. Grace filled me in on that, but that story's not over. Alex is planning on leaving town at the end of her apprenticeship, but Grace is keeping her hopes up that Alex will give Christopher a chance.

So when Cassandra calls me, I'm happier than if it were a head hunter on the other end of the line. I never met the woman, but somehow I kept the bag from her store—purple with the name of her shop in golden cursive.

It makes me feel good.

"I'm delighted to inform you that you have won our Valentine's Sweepstakes, and we'd like to invite you next weekend to claim your prize."

"A sweepstakes?" I don't remember entering a sweepstakes. But then again, lots happened that weekend. Maybe it was part of the V card. Maybe I put my name down somewhere.

"Mm-hmm," she says. "Are you available next weekend? The prize is a two-night stay in town, one dinner, a sleigh ride, and a gift card to spend in any or all shops of Emerald Creek. How does that sound?"

Are you kidding me right now? I giggle. "That sounds...exactly like what I need." No joke, I've been thinking of ditching everything here and settling in a small town. I don't need a boss, thank you very much. I know what I'm doing.

I'd need referrals to get my first jobs, and maybe Grace, Autumn, and the gang could help with that. And then it'd be word of mouth. I have faith in my capabilities. I might be clueless in the dating world, but professionally? I know my worth. Maybe this phone call is fate. "What do I need to do?"

"Pack your bags, and we'll see you Friday!" Cassandra answers.

I thank her, hang up, and immediately send a group text to the girls of Emerald Creek.

They respond with clapping and fireworks emojis, and we all plan to meet up on Friday at Lazy's.

"There you are!" Miss Angela grabs a key behind her, and motions me to follow her up the stairs.

I hope she's not taking me to the room I shared with Lucas on Valentine's Day. It's still too painful.

Too raw.

But we stop in front of the same door. It'd be rude to ask for another room, right? After all, I'm not paying for it. She donated it to the sweepstakes.

She doesn't know my situation or what went down with Lucas. How could she?

I just need to be thankful and suck it up.

She hands me the key and all but shoves me inside the room, quickly closing the door behind me.

I stay glued to the entrance, my bag heavy, my heart heavier, fresh memories slicing through me. My eyes water, the room goes blurry, and all I can see are rough shapes. The rocking chair in which he sat restless, convincing me to go out and enjoy the town. The reading nook where the sexy nightie he bought for me landed on his jeans.

The bed where he made me feel so treasured.

Everything is so fresh, so raw, so cruel. Even his scent assails me, my mind playing tricks on me.

I let my mouth curl down and my shoulders shake while tears run along my cheeks.

Why did I think coming back would be a good idea?

"What are you doing here?" The voice snaps like a whip, startling me.

My breath hitches, and my sobs die in my throat. I wipe my tears and widen my eyes at Lucas stepping out of the bathroom.

He looks like he's lost some weight. His hair is longer, and I can't help but notice how I love the way it curls around his ears. His eyes roam the length of my body. "The hell you doing in my room?"

His room?

Oh god. What is going on? I need to get out of here, and fast. Legs wobbly, I whip around to the door, but his hand closes around mine on the doorknob. "Thalia," he growls. "What is going on?" The low rumbling of his voice shoots straight down to my middle.

It's a mistake. A terrible mistake. He's here for the contract with the resort, no doubt, and Miss Angela got confused with the room assignment. It's understandable.

"If you talk to Lucas Hunt now, we'll have to press charges against you."

Oh god. The agony of his closeness, his heat, his scent, the vibration of his body inches from mine. How good it felt, back then, to be in his arms. How far away it seems now. Unattainable. Forbidden. "Let me go," I breathe. "Please."

"Not until you tell me what happened between us." He lifts my chin to face him, his fingers lingering for a beat. "And why you're here," he adds on an exhale, his breath so familiar, so delicious, I lose the ability to speak.

"Thalia," he nudges me.

"It's a—a mistake. Miss Angela got confused. I'm sure. I'll sort it out." I wiggle my hand on the doorknob, but that just prompts him to tighten his hold on me.

His gaze softens. "Thalia," he says again, pain and a reproach in his tone.

"I—I shouldn't be here. It's a mistake. Please don't tell Carla. Or anyone. I didn't mean to. I swear."

His eyebrows furrow. "The fuck are you talking about?"

I should be mad at him for what happened to me, but I can't be. When it comes to Lucas Hunt, I'm powerless.

It used to be scary.

Then it got delicious, for a few days.

Now it's dangerous for me. I could get in serious trouble.

I need to get a grip. I need to get through to him. Ohmygod this is not looking good.

I take a deep breath. "Carla and Heather—" I start.

"Heather?" he interrupts me.

I stammer. "H—Heather from HR. Th-they said I shouldn't t—talk to you or I'd get in more s—serious trouble. Look, I know d—deep down you're a good guy, Lucas. So do me a f—favor, and don't tell anyone you saw me, okay? I didn't mean to—o-obviously the room thing is a mix-up."

Lucas takes his hand off mine, only to engage the deadbolt. Then he takes both my hands in his and pulls me inside the room. "What are you talking about?" he says in a low voice as he sits on the bed, pulling me to him.

I pull my hands from his and take a step back. Lucas and me on a bed? No.

"Thalia. What are you talking about?" he repeats.

There's no way he doesn't know. Come on. But maybe he doesn't know *all* the details. Also, to be honest? It's frigging hard to head out the door with Lucas Hunt looking at me with smoldering eyes, saying my name in that voice, all but begging me to talk to him, *and* with the feel of his hands lingering on mine.

No one could resist that.

So I indulge him. I stupidly state the obvious. "I won the sweepstakes, but also my termination states I can't talk to you or else." I lick my lips, fighting the dryness in my mouth. This is torture.

His back straightens. "Your termination?"

"Y—yeah. I uh, you know."

His face hardens. "No. I don't know, Thalia." He pounces off the bed. "Why don't you tell me?" he nearly yells at me.

So I tell him.

And while I do, he paces around the room, running his hands through his hair, clenching his jaw, muttering swear words.

I guess maybe he didn't know.

Wow.

When I'm done, he roars, "Carla played her cards, and my uncle is an asshole. But he lied to me. Said you'd been given a nice package, great recommendations." His gaze cuts through me when he adds, "When you didn't show at the aquarium, I figured you were done with me." He blinks, pain etched in his features, and guilt washes over me for cutting him out. "I shoulda known something was up with the job. I didn't fight back enough for you."

He reaches for my nape, pulling me into him, fisting my hair. "He holds me by the balls, there's no other way to say it. I need this job with him, for Madison's health insurance. But that doesn't mean I won't fight this with you, Thalia."

The enormity of what he's saying is too much. I can't fight anyone. I can't even afford a lawyer. And he can't seriously be considering siding with me against his uncle.

But his hand sure feels good right where it is.

So when my phone dings, I ignore it.

"You need to take that?" he asks, and it doesn't escape me that his hand is still right there, pulling me into him, but he's not doing anything about it, keeping us close yet keeping the distance.

It's confusing and delicious at the same time.

"I'm meeting the girls at Lazy's tonight," I mumble. "I should get ready."

He lets go of my nape, and his eyebrows shoot up in surprise. "Oh yeah?" His panty-melting slow grin spreads on his face. "That's so cool, Thalia. You stayed in touch with them. I like that for you."

I blush under his gaze. "Yeah, we've been texting and...you know, I kept them in the loop." I pat my hair down. "I'm thinking of moving here," I blurt out. "I'll put some feelers out tonight, see if it's even feasible. If I would get enough work. I'm not getting any leads in the city."

His eyes dance with happiness. "That's a great idea. You'll fit right in in Emerald Creek. I knew it the minute we drove into town."

I can't help the smile that spreads on my face. "Yeah?"

"Yeah! I mean, what's not to like about this place? I'd move here in a heartbeat."

"You would?" It's not difficult to imagine Lucas in a place like Emerald Creek. He's down-to-earth, no bullshit, hard working. But he needs the job at his uncle's. Benefits and all that. I don't need to repeat that to him. It's bittersweet, the way he's happy for me while he's tied up in his own situation.

The way he's happy for me although we're no longer together.

I try to shake the sadness and grab my toiletries from my duffel bag. "I'm going to freshen up," I say as I walk into the bathroom.

I stop in my tracks. His toiletry bag is hanging on a hook. And in the shower, there's a three-in-one gel that claims to wash, condition, and hydrate men's hair and body. Water droplets trickle down the glass wall.

Right. I turn around and hit his muscular chest. "Um. There's been a mix-up in the rooms," I repeat my earlier obvious statement.

"Yeah." He rubs his chin. "You said something about a sweepstakes?"

I nod. "I won a sweepstakes. Why are *you* here?" I don't really want to talk about the resort's contract and hear which architect took over after me. It's a sore spot.

He smirks. "Same thing. Sweepstakes. Except I only came because my sister intercepted the message, and she wouldn't have let me live it down if I'd declined. She's here with me. I booked her another room."

I'm relieved he doesn't mention the contract. He's here for Emerald Creek. For his sister. For fun. He deserves it. So much. "Do you remember entering a sweepstakes?"

"Nope."

Ah. "Same. And the choice of this room..."

"Yup."

Is this a confusion or a setup? "Something's up."

His eyes dance on my face. "Something's definitely up."

My phone dings. It's Grace, confirming we're still on for drinks in a few minutes. "I'm going to be late."

"Get ready," he says, pointing to the bathroom. "I'll get out of here once you leave. Get myself another room."

Cold washes over me. Right. Of course. Another room. I mean, what else was I thinking? This is not a repeat of our first visit to Emerald Creek.

And also, the threat from Carla still holds, right? Or does it? I mean, what if...? If something happened with Lucas *again*.

God, we didn't talk about the rest, did we? Although we cleared the air and determined that Carla and Lucas's uncle were a bunch of liars, we skirted the topic of us.

Was there ever an us?

Again, so out of my depth here.

When I come out of the bathroom, smoky eyes, fluffed-out hair, a spritz of perfume (I need to do right by the girls who gave me a makeover not so long ago), Lucas's gaze does a quick sweep of my body, and I can't miss the hunger in his eyes. Warmth spreads through me, and I lower my eyes.

He closes the gap between us and lifts my chin. "We're not done, Talliebelle," he says in a low growl. His thumb swipes my jaw, and I lean into it.

God he feels good.

I wish I knew how to respond. What to ask, what to say. *Not done about what*? Is he talking about *us*? He is, right? Please make it be that.

When it comes to Lucas, I feel so powerless—in the best possible way.

Chapter Twelve

Thalia

The girls greet me with a group hug.

"You look great!"

"Ohmygod we missed you!"

"Love your blouse!"

And then, "I can't believe it." I told them I'd lost my job but not where Lucas fit in that—or didn't, as it turns out.

I slide into the booth just as Justin sets a bowl of poutine on the table. He gives me a side hug like we're best buds and takes our drink orders. "God, it's good to be back," I say when he's gone. "I missed this place! You guys are so lucky to be living here, you have no idea."

"Tell it to this one," Grace says, pointing at Alex. "She's still planning on going back to New York before summer."

"Hey! I have serious money running on her staying," Autumn says.

"Why would you want to do that?" Eeep! I'm being just as nosy as the rest of the people here.

Alex blushes slightly, and her gaze slides to the bar before setting back on me. The man who'd all but carried her out of here on Valentine's Day is sitting with his back to the room. He's broody, deep in conversation with Justin.

Grace leans into me and whispers, "That's my cousin, Christopher. He's the baker, and Alex is doing her apprenticeship with him. Well, we hope they're doing more than that, to be honest. Can't get a word out of those two."

"What's that?" Alex asks. "Did I hear my name?"

"Nope!" Grace says. "I was...uh...congratulating Thalia on winning the sweepstakes."

Autumn leans over the table and wiggles her eyebrows. "Where's the hot guy?"

"Um...at the hotel, I guess? We're not— we're not a couple, you know."

"Is that so?" a familiar voice says above me. I look up and see a woman in her late forties gazing at me with mischief. Her beautiful, bluish-purple hair flows around her shoulders, a stark contrast to her white coat. She pulls a chair and takes the high end of the table. "I'm Cassandra," she says.

"Yes! We spoke on the phone. Such a pleasure to meet you in person. And thank you for the sweepstakes." She frowns quizzically at me. "I mean, it was a sweepstakes, so I suppose I—we—won a legit 'drawing,'" I say, air-quoting the word, "but still..." Where am I going with this? Oh yeah. "So my friend and I"—Lucas is still my friend, right?—"we were wondering...and this isn't important, it's just a detail, really...but we just couldn't remember where or how we entered the sweepstakes."

Cassandra smiles back. Says nothing. Just takes a sip of the hot toddy that Justin placed in front of her.

The girls look between themselves, and then to Cassandra, and then to me. No one says anything.

"Not—not that it matters," I stutter. "We're just super thankful."

"Good," Cassandra smiles.

The awkwardness instantly disappears when a man about Cassandra's age, wearing a tweed jacket and dark jeans, stops by our booth. I recognize him. He was on the panel of executives at the resort I presented my project to two weeks ago. A lifetime ago. "Ladies," he says.

"Hey." Alex and Grace wave.

Autumn sits up. "Hello, Mr. Hayes."

I nod briefly. He probably doesn't remember me. They must have had half a dozen proposals. Too many faces to commit to memory.

"Well, if it isn't our general manager in the flesh," Cassandra says. "What brings you to the lowlands? Life got too boring at the resort? Looking for a little rough and tumble with the common people?" She lifts one shoulder and giggles, throwing her head back, seemingly pleased by her teasing.

"There's nothing common about you, Cassandra. I'd love to visit with you sometime."

"Hm? You know where to find me."

"Ah, but I don't have a reason to visit your lingerie store, unfortunately."

"Really?" Cassandra perks up at this, actually checks him out top to bottom and back up. The woman has *game*. And no shame. And she rocks it. "We need to take care of that. Do come to my shop." Holy sh…

"I will most definitely take you up on that," he answers her in a low voice. Then he clears his throat and turns to me. "Right now, I'm here to see Ms. Williams. Thalia, right?"

Um... "Yes?"

"Can I steal her for a second?" He doesn't wait for an answer before leading me to a quiet corner of the bar. "I heard you are no longer with Hunt. May I ask which firm managed to snag you?"

You're going to have to bullshit your way through this one, Thalia. "I'm looking at different options," I answer. That's not a lie, right?

His face brightens. "Interesting." He strokes his jaw pensively. "Let me be honest with you, we were blown away by your presentation. The redesign you imagined is exactly what we were going for, but better. When we asked Hunt for a more detailed scope of work, and they assigned us a different architect, the owners weren't too pleased. *I* wasn't pleased."

He's probably just fishing for information on the new architect. As much as I hate the idea that someone else will bring the project I designed to life, I need to think about my career first. I can't burn bridges. This is a small world. I need to stay professional. "I'm sure they'll do a wonderful job, Mr. Hayes."

"Jim, please. Oh, I'm sure they'd be just fine, but we don't want just fine. We want someone with a vision. We want *you*."

Wow. I try to keep it in, so I just nod. Bringing in a client could be a good negotiating point with a firm that would want to hire me. And there are a few things that Hunt and Carla didn't want in the final project, that I could bring back to make it even better.

"Have you ever thought of starting your own firm?" he asks.

Yes, a thousand times yes. But I can't replace Hunt Enterprises. "Hunt is a one-stop shop. They offer—"

He waves dismissively. "Plenty of good workers here. That fellow who was with you. He was lapping up every word you said, clearly as taken with your presentation as we were. He seems to know his way around buildings. Talked with our maintenance guy. What's his trade?"

"He's...he's a construction superintendent with Hunt Enterprises. He oversees jobs. But—"

Hayes throws his hands in the air. "Perfect! Let's you, or us, make him a better offer!"

Yeah, that's not going to work.

"Look," he says, lowering his voice. "I get that this is a lot to process, and I don't expect an answer right this minute. But think about it. You could set yourself up as an independent architect and hire your guy. We'd be your first client. There'd be a handsome deposit to offset starting costs—you know how much Hunt was going to charge. And there will be more projects in the future. We're thinking treehouse glamping alongside the lake, some renovations in town buildings for employee housing, and in a few years, timeshare cabins tucked away in the woods. Plenty of work for you, and a great way to get your name out there for other contracts."

I'd need to hire a couple of people. One or two maximum. The construction oversight is what I'm less comfortable with. But hey, Lucas could give me some pointers as to where to find the right people. He bitched enough about me not asking for help, earlier. "I'll think about it." I'll need a solid contract. Lawyers. The equity in my apartment could cover that, until the business starts making money.

"You're already thinking about it." He smiles.

Busted. "I'll have an answer next week." I smile back.

"Perfect."

I watch him walk to the bar, and my gaze stops on Lucas, with a younger woman by his side—clearly his sister, Madison, if the photo on his phone is anything to go by. She's beaming, sipping a glass of white wine, and he—

He's looking at me.

Staring.

His eyes boring into me.

And his mouth curves into a smile.

My heart does a happy dance, and I wave at him.

Minutes later, we're all sitting around two tables we pulled together. Alexandra and her broody baker are on opposite sides, but the looks between the two could set fire to the place. Cassandra and Jim Hayes are cozy next to each other, down the table from me. Whatever they're saying to each other gets lost in the loud conversation between Autumn and Grace and a couple other young women whose names I don't remember. Madison sits with them, her eyes dancing between the women. Grace's brother Colton, the mechanic who towed our car, joins us, and he immediately recognizes Lucas and slaps him on the back as if he were an old friend.

Lucas sits to my right. His plaid flannel shirt stretches on his forearms when he lifts his beer to his lips, and his grin all but melts me. He leans over and whispers in my ear, "I missed you."

The turmoil of the past few weeks, the feeling of betrayal, the panic over my tanking career, all has disappeared in the last couple of hours.

All that remains is a future I can design for myself. A future where he'd look damn good. I meet his gaze and clink my bottle to his. "I missed you too."

We're not done, Thalia, he said to me earlier.

I don't want to be done.

But he won't be able to take the offer, will he? That'd be crazy. And then there's Madison. She has a life in the city. He wouldn't want to uproot her, and she still needs him.

Justin and a waitress bring plates to share for the table—two cheese and charcuterie boards, more poutine, nachos, open face grilled cheese sandwiches cut into bite size pieces. They both pull chairs to join us. We start digging in.

I glance at Madison, sitting opposite and to my left, laughing hysterically at something one of the women just said, which makes Grace roll her eyes and Cassandra join in the laughter.

Lucas reaches over me for a nacho, his scent a sweet memory. "What did Jim Hayes want?" he says in my ear, then plops the nacho in his mouth.

I take a long pull of my beer. "He made me an offer." When do I tell Lucas about his place in Hayes's offer?

He fist pumps. "Yes. God I want to kiss you right now."

I can't help but laugh. I feel like being kissed too. "Then why don't you?"

He lowers his voice and gets closer to me. "This is a PG-rated bar, Thalia."

I turn my face to him, and we're so close I can smell the fresh beer on his breath. "There are PG-rated kisses, you know."

He leans over, cups my shoulders in his strong arm, and leaves a tender kiss on my temple. "I know, darling. I just don't trust myself around you yet."

I pinch my lips to stifle the smile that spreads from my mouth to my entire body.

"It's okay, let it go," he says, pulling me against him.

And I do. I chuckle softly and let him rock me against his hard body. He kisses my hair and says, "So. Sleigh ride tomorrow?"

Oh yeah. Damn. That sounds dangerously romantic. "Madison is coming, right?"

He grins. "She'd love that, but don't think I don't know what you're doing."

I clench my thighs. "I'm meeting the family," I breathe.

He squeezes my shoulder. "I like that. But dinner? That's just you and me, baby. Tomorrow night. Just you and me."

Chapter Thirteen

Thalia

I toss and turn all night, thinking about the evening's events.

About Hayes's offer. About the evening with the girls at the bar. About how everything in Emerald Creek felt like home. The way everyone welcomed me back like an old friend.

But mostly, I think about Lucas. About the night we spent here in this room. Scorching hot.

I think about his arm around my shoulders. About his feather, PG kisses. Tender and sweet.

Was he just teasing? I know he was genuinely happy about the offer I received from the resort. But did his display of affection mean more, or was it just him being the good guy he is?

I don't trust myself around you yet. Does that mean he wants to get to a point where he no longer wants me? A point where we are just friends?

I fall asleep as the sky loses its inkiness and the stars begin to fade, and wake up close to noon to a light snow steadily falling. The landscape outside my window is gorgeous in a soft and cozy way.

It's a perfect day for a sleigh ride.

I grab a chocolate croissant at the bakery. Christopher, the baker, is helping out at the register, and I get a chance to see him up close. Man, he's sexy. I sure hope he and Alex solve their issues, whatever they are. She's a sweet girl, and she deserves her HEA.

On my way out, I stop on the steps of the bakery, tearing out the flaky, buttery croissant with my fingers. I eat it while admiring how this Victorian house has been lovingly maintained. As far as I can tell from my station on the wraparound porch, no chipping paint, no sign of rot or decay, despite the brutal winters.

From this slightly elevated vantage point, I again note the variety of architectural styles represented around The Green. Federalist, Greek Revival, Colonial, Georgian, and more, with variations reflecting the creativity of their owners. For our sleigh ride, we're meeting at the white steeple church that stands on the smaller side of the Green, next to Main Street.

I lick chocolate off my fingers as the sleigh approaches. Lucas and Madison exit the library, and my heart flutters at the way he rolls his shoulders, at the confidence in his gait as he strolls down the sidewalk. He oozes strength and power.

Of course he does.

He's a carpenter by trade. A construction manager. His hands and experience are what make works like mine come to life. A deep heat settles in my center as I quickly make my way to them.

There's way more to our connection than one hot night together. How did I not see that earlier? And why do I have to see that now that it's no longer within my reach?

"Thalia!" Madison hugs me like a long-lost friend. "Don't you love this place?" She lets go of me and swirls around like a little girl, her arms wide open.

Lucas chuckles, and so does the young man who hops down from the sleigh. "You guys ready? I'm Hunter," he says.

Madison does a double take at Hunter, bats her eyelashes, then turns to start petting the horse. Or maybe to hide her blush. "What's his name?" she asks Hunter. "I'm so sorry we're putting you to work," she tells the horse.

"Her name is Sunshine, and she loves being outside." Sunshine neighs, Madison squeals, and Hunter laughs. "She really wants to get going."

"Let's go then." Lucas holds my elbow to help me up, and Madison follows. Lucas hops in, picks his sister up, and plops her on his other side, his thick thigh warm against mine. Oh god, sweet torture.

"Um. Can I get the middle?" Madison asks.

"No."

"I'm scared!" She narrows her eyes at him. "It's not my fault."

"Then now's your chance to get off. I get the middle seat." Lucas takes the heavy blanket Hunter hands us, pulls it over our knees, and grabs my hand under it.

Well. Okay then.

"Ugh! You're so mean," Madison grumbles.

I feel bad for Madison. Is it the memory of the accident that scares her?

"She can sit up front," Hunter says.

Madison blushes again. The rider's seat is way up high, and with two of them, there won't be much more space than down here. She looks at Lucas as if to ask for permission. He shrugs.

She hops to the front. Hunter wraps a blanket around her shoulders and over her knees. She turns around and winks at me, a devious little smile spreading on her face.

Lucas smiles. "All it took was a guy. Why am I paying for therapy?" Then he scooches away from me to spread himself out where Madison was just sitting.

And pulls me with him, his hand snug over my shoulder, my head inside the crook of his arm.

So good.

We leave the village in a jingle of bells, go under the covered bridge, and slide up the hill on a narrow trail. The cold wind slaps my face. Lucas leans over me and pulls the blanket up to my chin. "You okay?" he asks.

"It's magical." White farms and red barns and split rail fences dot the countryside. A dog barks joyfully at us.

"Yeah, it sure is," he answers. But his gaze is on me.

We come to a flat, open space. There's a lone cow in the snow, looking at us. Is that...?

"That's your friend!" Hunter laughs. "Daisy!" he calls out.

Lucas and I both start laughing.

Hunter turns to Madison and says a few words that are lost in the wind. She nods, and he pushes Sunshine into a gallop.

Daisy starts running parallel to us in the field, her body rocking front and back. She kicks her hind legs a couple of times before giving up the race. At least she didn't cross in front of us.

Madison squeals and nests herself against Hunter.

"Guy knows how to talk to her," Lucas says.

Once Daisy is far behind us, Hunter slows our pace to a gentle trot. Alongside the trail, a brook meanders between trees laden with thick snow. I snuggle deeper in the blanket, committing this perfect moment to memory.

Suddenly, cold air runs down my back as Lucas leans over to peek at Madison and Hunter. His eyes bug out. "I think she's driving." I jut my chin out, curious. Sure enough, Madison is holding the reins, Hunter next to her talking in her ear.

"That's great," I say.

"No. That's a miracle." He leans back in the seat, pulling me back against him. He kisses my hair softly. "Madison was driving," he whispers against my ear. "When they had the accident. Never wanted to be behind the wheel again."

I gasp and stare at Madison. Poor girl. She must be dealing with so much trauma and unnecessary guilt. I can't imagine what she's been through. What Lucas has been through, trying to help her.

And I'm beyond moved that Lucas is sharing this intimate information with me.

The sleigh gains momentum as we go down the hill. Madison's gloved fingers clench around the reins, but Hunter sets one hand on hers and one around her shoulders. "Let her gain speed, she'll need the momentum to go up the hill," he says, loud enough for us to hear.

Lucas's gaze is fixed on his sister, eyes shiny, pride oozing from him.

The sleigh dips and hiccups as we hit the bottom of the slope and slide back up. Madison squeals, then erupts in happy laughter, throwing her head back.

"Good girl, Sunshine," Hunter says, taking back the reins. "You too," he adds, turning to Madison.

I giggle, and Lucas kisses my hair again.

Then trails down.

To my cheek.

To my neck.

Finds the spot where the hickey used to be.

Looks up at me for permission, and when he likes what he sees, proceeds to give me another.

I roll my head back and buck my hips up to meet his wandering hand.

He growls. "We better stop."

He's right, so we stop.

Then he growls again. "Your room or mine tonight?"

My heart stops, then starts with a flutter. Then bangs in my ribcage.

He tucks my hair behind my ear. "Why so shocked? Told you I wasn't done with you."

Okay. Last time, sleeping with Lucas didn't end so well for me. The night was great, mind you. It's the consequences. What could possibly go wrong this time? What am I missing?

"Stop thinking, Talliebelle. You nearly came from my mouth on your neck right now. Let go."

Well, there was also your hand between my legs, to be exact.

"What now?"

What?

"You're still thinking. Stop thinking." He cups my chin in his fingers and kisses my lips softly.

Madison's laughter cuts through our moment. "Oh, don't mind us," she says. I pop my eyes open. We're back in front of the church. Madison and Hunter are on either side of Sunshine. Madison's gaze shifts between Lucas and me. Hunter's gaze is all over Madison.

Lucas's lips are still on mine. I push softly on his chest, but he keeps me there with one strong arm around my back and growls. His eyes are half-closed, a frown between his eyebrows, and damn if that isn't the swooniest feeling. To see him lost in his moment kissing me.

He lets go of me but dips back for a quick kiss on my lips. Then he folds the blanket and jumps down. He stretches his arms out and catches me, then sets me on the sidewalk and discreetly hands Hunter a tip.

"That was so much fun!" Madison says. She goes to Sunshine and pets her. She seems to have no intention of leaving.

Lucas stretches. "Maddie bee, you're going to be on your own, tonight. Thalia and I have business to discuss."

She cocks an eyebrow. "Business, yeah, right. No offense, Thalia," she says to me, lowering her voice like we're having a private conversation. "I like you for him, I really do. I just don't like it when he treats me like a baby." She turns back to her brother. "Just say you're on a date with your girlfriend!"

"What—I..." Lucas is at a loss for words. Interesting.

"It's about time you had a girlfriend," she huffs.

My eyes dart between them. Lucas without girlfriends? Hard to believe.

"You have hookups..." Madison clarifies for all to hear. As a matter of fact, Cassandra materializes out of nowhere and joins our little group. "*Lots* of hookups..." Madison adds, rolling her eyes.

Okay, TMI. Can we please move on?

"...It's about time you had a girlfriend," she repeats. She looks at her brother with authority. Like she's his mother. He looks down and shuffles his feet. He might have been her guardian, but they were both so young when their parents passed. They've both parented each other through their young adult age, and it's poignant and sad and beautiful to witness in that moment.

"You shouldn't be alone tonight, Madison," I say, not bearing the idea. "We can discuss this business some other time." Because there actually *is* business I want to talk about with him.

"A bunch of us are going to The Growler tonight," Hunter says. He's drinking Madison in, and she blushes at his words. "You're welcome to come. If you'd like."

"Oh great!" Madison says with a little spring in her feet.

He turns to Lucas. "If that's cool with you."

"The Growler?" Lucas asks, and I can feel Madison's frustration mounting.

She is, by my calculations, twenty-one. Maybe not a full-on adult in Lucas's eyes, but definitely no longer a child.

Lucas's gaze darts between Hunter, Madison, and me.

"It's a hangout place out in the hills," Cassandra informs us. "They have live music, pool tables, bar areas. Grace and her friends usually hang out there on Saturdays. They'll keep an eye out for Madison. Not that there's anything to worry about. She'll be in good hands with Hunter."

Hunter sticks his hands in his pockets and nods his thanks to Cassandra. "I should get going. I'll pick you up later?"

Chapter Fourteen

Lucas

I'm broken over what happened to Thalia. The way she lost her job? I should have done something. I should have reached out to her. See how she was doing.

Tell her I missed her.

Fuck I missed her.

She was alone. Bullied. Terrified. And I didn't show up for her.

How do I make it right?

But now we're having dinner, and I'm going to try and be in the moment.

Thalia bites her bottom lip and twirls her wine in her glass, catching the lights of the fire burning in the massive stone hearth. Dinner is at a small, cozy place in town, so we walked. There are white tablecloths and crystal chandeliers and thick carpets on the massive flagstones. Waiters and waitresses dressed in black slacks and crisp white shirts refill our glasses and bread plates and set out an infinite succession of delicate bites that compose the tasting menu. I'm only hungry for Thalia.

"So, there's something I need to ask you," Thalia says, her gaze lifting to me. She's not trying to turn me on, I know she's not, but damn if I don't get uncomfortably hard when she looks up at me like that.

Or maybe it's because she needs to ask me something?

"What is it, Talliebelle." I resist the urge to take her hand in mine. I need to make the world feel good again for her. But I know she's fiercely independent, so I need to hold back on the Knight-in-Shining-Armor attitude. Yeah, I go to therapy too, sometimes on my own, sometimes with Madison, and that's what the therapist calls it so I can get it through my thick head.

Not every woman wants a Knight in Shining Armor.

But what if she *needs one?* My Inner Knight screams back. *I* am *him!*

"Hayes is encouraging me to set up my own firm. Their deposit would fund my start-up costs..."

I saw the guy talk to her at the pub and had a good feeling about it. "Fuck, Thalia, that's...that's incredible! You're saying yes, right?"

She sighs. "That's where I'd need your help."

My stomach bottoms out, and my dick perks up. I guess my therapist hasn't met Thalia yet, a woman of contradictions.

God, I love her.

"What do you need my help with?" I focus on sounding casual. Not desperate. Not elated.

"They would want my firm to oversee construction." She lets the words sink in. That's three levels deeper than *We want you to continue the project.* "Now, I can hire people to help on the design side. I know where to find them, and I know who to look for. From what he said, money wouldn't be a problem. I could attract them with a great pay and benefits package. But construction? I wouldn't know where to begin. I don't have the right network. I wouldn't know what skill set to look for, how to set up interviews. If there even are interviews when it comes to construction, or if it's all referrals and word of mouth. That scares me, Lucas. That could tank my business. Would you know someone I could trust with that? Someone who wouldn't mind relocating here during the project?"

Heat spreads through my chest. Why isn't she asking me directly? Does she really think I would let some fucker mess up with her vision? Not to mention, work for her? Be close to her? Hell, I've wanted to work on her projects from the very beginning. That's one of the main reasons I schemed to have my uncle send me with her to Emerald Creek. Okay, not the main reason.

I wanted an in with her, and boy did I get it.

Then it was all ruined.

And now she's bringing it back to me, just a million times better.

"Yeah, I know just the guy." I let go of her hand. I don't want to come across as controlling. I rub my hands on my thighs. Set myself back in my chair.

"Yeah?" She doesn't get it yet.

"Uh-huh."

"Just like that? How—how is he? How do you know we'll be a good fit?"

"I know because he's been in love with the way your mind works from the day he met you. I know because the idea of bringing your designs to life is what gets him out of bed in the morning. I know because ever since he realized you lost your job because of something he did, he's been torturing himself over how to make it right. And I know because the idea of working by your side, under your guidance, helping you thrive and build beautiful buildings, just gave a new purpose to his life." I don't trust my hands right now, but boy do I need a drink.

Thalia gapes at me. "But—but…"

"But what?"

"Madison?" she blurts out.

"What about her?" Thalia had mentioned benefits, hadn't she? So what was the hold up?

"She needs you."

"Not as much as I'd like to think. It might be good for her to be on her own. Although, she's been ranting on and on about Emerald Creek, she might just move—"

Hold on here.

I grab her hand. "Wait. Are you saying yes?"

"Ohmygod, yes! Of course, yes!" she shrieks as she stands and lands on my lap, hugging me.

"Awww, did he propose?" a woman sitting at a nearby table asks.

My heart swells as Thalia turns to her. "Almost," she says.

"How does that work, an almost proposal?" the man counters.

I bore my gaze into Thalia's and say low enough so only she hears me, "Take two complicated people who want different things out of life."

"Throw them in a bedroom together," Thalia continues in an equally low, only-for-me tone.

"And a few weeks later—voila! An almost proposal," I finish in a growl before kissing her deeply under the patrons' applause.

"Do we really want different things out of life?" she asks as we walk back to our bed-and-breakfast, concern in her voice.

I stop us in our tracks and bring her body against mine, lacing my arm around her waist. "You want to be independent, to create, and to thrive. I want to help you, make your dreams come true, and protect you. So yes, we want different things, my Talliebelle. Different things that bring us together like two magnets." I kiss her deeply again. Her mouth yields to mine more openly now that we're shrouded in the darkness of the night. "Now, an important question."

She looks up at me, eyebrows furrowed.

"Your room or mine?"

We end up in her room, and only because it was closer to the entrance. We lock the door and shuck off our shoes, I throw condoms on the nightstand, and then we're at each other's clothes, tearing them off.

But when I find her naked and warm against me, her legs circling my hips, I hoist her up and kiss her softly.

And then...

I take. My. Time.

Because it's not three months I'm going to have with her, it's a lifetime. I know it in my bones. I know it my veins.

I know it in my heart and soul.

And I am going to savor every moment with her.

I set her softly on the bed and trail kisses on her feet, sucking on her toes. She plops herself on her elbows and laughs, little rivers of giggles that hit my stomach and warm my chest.

And then her giggles turn to soft pants as I lick my way up her calves, round her knees, inside her thighs. Her greedy hands pull on my hair as I approach her sweet center. Her moans become frustrated as I skirt her folds and suckle on her belly button. Lick my way up her breastbone.

Her symphony of sounds picks up again as I find one breast and worry it with my mouth. Her writhing hips find my cock, teasing precum out of it.

The need to be inside her is almost irresistible.

Almost.

The need to have her beg for me is stronger.

I move on to her adorable face, cupping it in both hands. Her gaze bores into mine, dark pools in which I drown. I lick her lips, and she opens her mouth, taking me hungrily in. Her hands pull me stronger into her, then her fingers trail down my back, until her nails graze my ass as she pulls me against her. She hooks her thighs around my hips again, positions her entrance right against my cock, and moans.

I break the kiss and rub our noses together.

"Lucas..."

"Mmm?"

"What are you doing?"

Sweet Thalia. "Making love to you?"

She chuckles, and her belly moving under me almost makes me come. "When are you going to take me?"

"Aah, that." I flip her around on her belly, and she squeals in surprise.

And then she tilts her ass up and looks at me over her shoulder, biting her lip, lowering her eyes. "So that's how you like it, huh?"

"I heard no complaints last time. But I like it any which way."

She flips back on her back, pushes me on my heels, unwraps a condom, sheathes me, and straddles me. All in one swift motion.

The woman knows what she wants.

And she wants me.

"Yessss," she says as she finally, finally takes my cock inside her. I'm big, and I know last time I wasn't gentle at first, but she's not slow or hesitant. She takes her pleasure with me, her tits bouncing in my face, pants turning into moans as a thin sheen of sweat glistens on her skin, and god there's nowhere else I want to be.

Ever.

She clenches around me and rides her orgasm, eyes rolling back, my name on her lips, her nails digging into my shoulders. Before she's done, I buck my hips and join her.

She's so fucking beautiful.

So perfectly mine.

And so it begins...

ALEXANDRA

Two weeks later

"Hey." The warm voice glides over me like sunshine. "There you are."

I turn around to face Christopher and my breath catches. I should be used to it by now, but the effect he has on me grows every day.

It's not just the way he looks. Yeah, sure, I'm not immune to the fact that he's tall and tan, with dark curls I want to run my fingers through. That he has a body built by years of lifting heavy stuff for work—wide shoulders, narrow hips, biceps straining his shirts.

When he has his shirt on. My apprenticeship at the bakery comes with room and board in the house he shares with his daughter, and I've accidentally seen him bare chested, once or twice. Let me tell you, those memories are burned in my brain.

All this is fine. But.

It's the way he looks *at me*. With attentiveness. Interest. Care. Making sure I'm alright.

Like right now. "You okay?" he asks, his eyes dancing on me. Dark, soft eyes. Registering concern.

"Yeah, I'm fine," I breathe and step aside.

We're in the large kitchen-slash-den in the back of the bakery. It's where we are most of the time when we're not baking. I find my training manual, sit at the farmhouse table, and pretend to reread my last notes.

"I was worried," he says.

Worried? "Why?"

"You just up and left. Didn't take your phone." He walks up to me until I feel his presence at my back.

"I brought a welcome basket to Thalia and Lucas. A loaf of Three Millers, apple muffins, and a maple pie."

"That's really nice, Alexandra. So like you." He leans his hip against the table, close to me. I keep my eyes on my workbook. "I've said it before, and I'll say it again. Food brings people together. And your maple pie? Spot on. I tasted your batch. The dough was perfect. Good call, bringing them that."

Oh no no no. No early morning compliments from my hot boss, please.

He moves to the kitchen counter. "How are they settling in?"

Well, Thalia had sex hair, and Lucas showed up behind her at the door with nothing but a flannel pajama bottom. "They looked great."

"Good," he says softly, then, "happy for them."

"He was making coffee," I say.

And then—get this—I blurt, "I think they'd just had sex."

Why did I say that? Granted, they'd totally just had sex. Thalia was wrapped in a robe, like I said, she had sex hair, and also her cheeks were rosy, and there was a glow about her. You could just *tell*. Lucas, I didn't see too much of—and thank god for that—except that he asked if I wanted to come in for coffee. *No thank you.*

Ohmygod I need to change the topic. "He asked if I wanted coffee," I add to try and deflect. "I said no." Like I need to say that? Of course I would say no! Who wants to have after-sex coffee with a new couple?

I should just shut up.

Christopher hands me a steaming cup of coffee. "Well, I got you one out of the two." I look up at him, see his half grin, his eyes dancing on me, and it's all I can do to keep it together. My belly goes all to mush, and my center is on fire, and I need my two hands to grab the coffee without touching Christopher's fingers and bring it down to the tabletop without spilling it.

He sits across from me, his own coffee in hand.

We sip in silence.

His coffee tastes amazing. Of course it does.

The awkwardness recedes.—I think.

"Bringing welcome baskets to new residents, huh?" he says after a while. "You're a real small-town girl now." His gaze roams from my eyes to my hairline to my throat, as if to check that all of me is, indeed, small-town.

"I don't know about that," I whisper. I love living in Emerald Creek, and I'll be heartbroken when I have to go back to New York, but there's no way I can stay here. I've been clear about this to Christopher, but he brings it up occasionally.

His mouth curls up in a side grin. "Oh, but I do. You just need to own it. Own who you are. What you want." He leans over the table to tuck a stray hair behind my ear. "And tell me."

I almost lean into his strong hand, willing it to cup my whole face. If only I could let myself go, I could have that. Maybe not what Thalia and Lucas have, but close enough.

But I'm paralyzed, fearing the consequences.

You see, I've been keeping a part of my life secret. Something that will make Christopher hate me when he finds out.

And he will find out.

And when he does…

He'll end me.

Afterword

One Night In Emerald Creek is a novella written as a short introduction to the world of Bella Rivers' books.

If you loved the small town quirkiness of Emerald Creek, want to know if Daisy and Ms. Angela are still playing tricks on people, and if Justin, Chris, Alex, Grace and many others get their happy ever after, then the Emerald Creek series of books is for you.

Read Never Let You Go, Alexandra and Christopher's story, here (scan) :

About the author

Bella Rivers writes steamy small town romances with a guaranteed happily ever after, and themes of found family and forgiveness. Expect hot scenes, fierce love, and strong language!

A hopeless romantic, Bella is living her own second chance romance in the rolling hills of Vermont. When she's not telling the stories of the characters populating her dreams, you can find her baking, hiking, skiing, or just hanging around her small town to soak in the happiness.

Her newsletter is where Bella shares progress on her writing as well as sneak peeks into upcoming books, the occasional recipe from her characters, and books from other writers she thinks her readers might like. Subscribe from her website, www.bellarivers.com.

You can also connect with Bella on TikTok, Instagram, or Facebook, all @bellariversauthor, or through the contact form on her website.

Made in United States
Orlando, FL
14 September 2025